Love Fumbles 3:
A Reflective Novel
About A University Student In 1970s Alabama

By Regina N. Smith

For Ken and Lillie

Prologue

Losing her inhibitions, twenty-two-year-old Nancy Perkins lingered within the tall, metallic phone booth. It was 3:40 pm, a few minutes after her final class of the day. She was in her final semester at South Louisiana University in Wood Oak, Louisiana. What would have been a remarkable time in her life, Nancy wanted to share it with someone special from her past. She had been offered a job at Wood Oak High, her old high school, upon graduation. Her friends had planned on giving her a celebratory dinner in her honor. Yet, the person she wanted there most of all, she knew wasn't aware of the special occasion.

Scraping her fingers through her brown hair, Nancy pondered, *maybe he would be home this time*. She prayed for her wish to come true: to hear the soothing voice of the hunk that had the memorable smile, grey eyes, and handsome laugh that often preoccupied her thoughts. That person was Paul James Boudreaux, who, unfortunately, was no longer a part of her life. Yet, Nancy was hopeful and appreciative to have the small piece of paper in her hands given to her by the girlfriend of a mutual friend, providing a possible reconnection.

Nancy listened to the anxious tone of the phone ringing, which mimicked her distraught heart. The young woman's dark blue eyes were anxious as she began to tap one of her brown boots against the floor. She brushed her sweaty hands against her brown miniskirt and tugged at her mauve colored top that rested underneath a gold and purple necklace.

The phone continued to ring, unanswered, like her previous attempts earlier that day.

He's still not home, Nancy thought with a heaviness to her body. She hung up the phone, left the booth, and gazed at the white cumulus clouds floating in the serene, deep blue sky.

When the woman would call later in the evenings, there had been a feminine greeting such as, "hello" or "Boudreaux residence," which resulted in an immediate departure on Nancy's end. Her earlier attempted phone calls were always unanswered. For once, Nancy wished that Paul himself would answer, but so far, he never did, dampening her spirits. Still, her friends had guaranteed that one day Paul would answer himself and hopefully, not his wife.

Nancy's upset eyes fell upon the golden engagement ring that had been placed upon her finger, wishing she had said *no* to the person who had given it to her. She finally had *a* ring, although not from the person that she genuinely wanted. The ring on her finger belonged in the trash, same as the man who had placed it there. *Why* and *how* things had gotten far between Nancy and *its betrothed* plagued her with a revulsion that made her stomach become agitated, wishing she could switch places with Paul's wife. If anyone deserved to be with him, why couldn't it have been her instead? Nancy exited the booth and reentered the front passenger side of her friend's vehicle, unsure of what to do next.

Chapter 1
Paul
1974

It was a sunny day in Camellia, Alabama, a beautiful community known for its scenic tree tunnels, antebellum homes, and mystic societies. Its Ivy League school, Camellia University, was recognized for its School of Medicine and School of Business. Most attending students were legacies who had a long-standing history and complex inner circles. One of the attending students was Paul James Boudreaux, a twenty-two-year-old handsome man with short black hair, captivating grey eyes, and a remarkable smile. He wore a plaid yellow and grey shirt, blue jeans, and brown leather shoes. Decades ago, Paul's father, Andrew Boudreaux, had graduated from the university's School of Business and his maternal grandfather, Beau Dupont, previously served as one of the university's board of directors when the university first opened its doors in the late 1800s. It had been a few weeks since completing his monthly reserve duties at the nearby armory that had resulted in a shift back to his focus on his family and scholarly obligations at the university.

Paul leaned with his arm propped against the wall to the hallway of the T. Tilberson School of Business. He was waiting by the office that belonged to Professor Kingsley, a man who also served as his academic advisor.

"Paul," Professor Kingsley said hurriedly, carrying his brown leather briefcase, "I need to see you in my office after our class tomorrow."

Paul began to wonder why. Professor Kingsley's class was Paul's last class of the day and the professor's last-minute request could cause the young father to be late to pick up his daughter from the daycare center. Paul contemplated calling his wife, Nell, but he remembered that she had a lot of afternoon and evening classes that day.

Geeze! Paul prayed that the appointment would not last long because the professor had been known to ramble extensively.

"Yes, sir," Paul answered, a heavy sigh escaping his lips.

Looking at his watch, Paul remained at the professor's closed door, tapping his foot with growing impatience.

"I couldn't have plagiarized my paper, Professor Kingsley," an anxious student argued, briskly walking behind Professor Kingsley in the hallway. "What evidence is there that I've done such a thing? None, whatsoever! I have two of the five books I borrowed from the library that I used in my research paper. I would like to see how I didn't cite my sources!"

Professor Kingsley had his briefcase in one hand and a handful of papers in the other. The man had dark brown eyes behind a pair of glasses, a blue tie, a brown jacket that covered a white shirt, brown pants, and black shoes. His head was balding with remnants of short salt and pepper hair.

"You need to lower that bass in your voice," Professor Kingsley warned the disgruntled student as they made their way down the hallway, walking past other students who were standing or moving in the opposite direction. There was visible tension in the professor's neck, arms, and shoulders. His jaw was clenched as he ignored everyone else in the hallway, shifting his papers under his arms so he could locate his jacket pocket for a key to unlock his office door. After obtaining the key, Professor Kingsley unlocked the door and entered the office with the angry student. He shut the door behind them, not acknowledging Paul as he waited outside of the professor's office.

Who is that wise guy, and why did Professor Kingsley ignore me? So much for showing up and wanting to leave as soon as possible. Paul pondered whether he should leave and return the next day, as he examined his watch again. What would have been a ten-minute head start would now become a twenty-minute drive from campus, due to the usual heavy afternoon traffic of cars leaving campus mixed with other drivers leaving to go home for the day.

Paul could hear some muffled arguing from the other side of the office door. He was glad that it wasn't him. He had enough of his fair share of lectures and arguments. Five minutes later, the door was opened with the upset student departing the office.

"It's not fair," the student said, his voice distressed. "It was a simple mistake that anyone could have made! Why can't I get a second chance to redo my paper?"

Paul cautiously stood by until the professor informed him to enter the office. Paul entered and closed the door behind himself. He slipped into a chair across from the professor's wooden desk. On the top of the desk were two tall piles of ungraded papers, two thick opened books with fine print, a cup of writing utensils, and a picture frame that exhibited an image of the professor and his smiling family. The office was small with wooden walls that held framed copies of Professor Kingsley's degrees in business and business administration.

"Sorry about that, Paul" Professor Kingsley stated, using a handkerchief to wipe sweat from his balding head. "I wanted to discuss a crucial observation regarding your progress at the university. We both understand that you enrolled while in the marine corps reserves. Initially, during your first semester, your grades were dismal, almost on the edge of academic probation."

An inkling of shame radiated from Paul's core, recalling some of what occurred. His eyes became distant.

A year ago, Paul had completed his military duties, but all that was left was a deeply troubled man. He had hoped that his enrollment at the university would provide a positive outcome. In a twist of events, he discovered himself experimenting with LSD, overindulging in alcohol, shagging random women on campus, and doing whatever it took to quickly forget his troubles.

Paul knew it was wrong but chose to go through the motions anyway. Why not? It was rationalized that he had done what he considered to be the right thing before, but still, he lost the people and the life he loved. What difference did it make? Nice guys always finished last, and he had been foolish to have been one, like some chump, knowing the outcome. He didn't care much about anything: being placed on academic probation, getting kicked out the university, the possibility of overdosing, his failing health…nothing… Yet, it all changed when Paul ran into a woman, he barely remembered shagging at a party. She informed him that he may need to be checked at a clinic because she had contracted gonorrhea and needed to undergo treatment.

Stunned, fearful, and irate, Paul immediately went to a clinic. It was humiliating to sit in a lobby with other people, questioning if they pondered not only their status, but his as well.

Two men in their early twenties sat beside each other two rows away from Paul. One appeared to be in greater distress than the other, almost on the verge of tears.

"I'm scared, man," the distraught one told his friend. "Why me? I don't deserve for this to happen! I always try to be picky with who I get with, but this broad had a bump down there, sayin' it was a pimple! Who has pimples on their vagina?"

The man's friend kept silent. He folded his arms across his chest, and slowly shook his head.

Across from the pair was a young couple seated together. The woman was red in the face while the guy next to her was getting paler with pleading eyes. Four seats away was an older man with a worried look on his face. He was in the process of biting a fingernail when a staff member motioned for him to follow her into another room.

Tossing his head back at his own problem, Paul's face became pinched with squinted eyes. His heart began to race, thinking how stupid he was to have put himself in such a predicament. He began praying and negotiating with God until one of the medical staff brought him into a backroom. Paul was tested and informed that he must be treated for gonorrhea, causing him to be horrified. After undergoing treatment and being cured, he decided that he needed to clean up his act, fast. If that was what it was like on the other end of the pendulum, he desired no part of it. Instead, when he felt depressed or overwhelmed, he would take himself to places that he liked, listen to records, hang out with friends, or take long drives. Eventually, his second semester grades improved. On his third semester, his journey of redemption continued. Then, Paul received a special letter.

"This semester," Professor Kingsley continued, his tone becoming more upbeat, "you've maintained an A-B average and remained vigilant on cleaning up your act. I wanted to continue to see how things are faring because whatever is going on, I hope it lasts."

"A lot has happened," Paul said, a slow smile building. "I decided to make a few positive changes...and reunited with the love of my life and got my little girl back. Life has been amazing, more than anything I could possibly say I deserve... My family keeps me wanting to do better for myself and for them as well, giving me a greater purpose in life."

"That's good to hear, Paul," the instructor said, leaning back into his chair with a wide grin. "I usually hear the opposite...This woman must truly be someone special, along with your child, of course. I've seen a change in you, for the better. During our first few encounters, you seemed to be quieter, almost withdrawn. I assumed it must have been due to finding it difficult to transition back into civilian life, but then again, that could have been something added. You seem much happier, you've been actively participating in class discussions, taking leadership roles in assignments, and your grades have skyrocketed in comparison to previous semesters. Keep up the good work, young man. I expect more great things to come."

"Thank you, sir," Paul said, giving Professor Kingsley a firm handshake. He departed the office with a swift vigilance to his core as he took a deep breath. Paul walked into the parking lot and got into his well-kept blue four-door vehicle that he nicknamed Wilma.

Wilma was a smooth ride with a deep blue paint job, bench seats, a car radio, and white wall tires. She was a beauty that Paul loved to show off and take nice long drives with his wife in search of new roads they had yet to explore together. The young man slid into his prized ride, turning on the engine and radio. A lively tune began to play, calming Paul of any left-over worries while he began to drive the familiar route. The traffic was there, but it didn't last as long as he expected once the other cars began to accelerate. Paul made a left turn two miles down the road, ending his short-lived role in the line of cars.

When he arrived at the Madonna Lily Daycare Center, Paul was relieved to discover that he was not the only late parent. There were three other vehicles in the parking lot. Two were empty and the other had a woman opening the back right passenger door to allow a young boy to enter.

Paul parked Wilma, climbed the stairs to the building, and entered. A woman who Paul assumed to be the other parent was talking to one of the women who worked at the daycare. Three children, including Paul's four-year-old daughter, Sharon Boudreaux, were lounging near the wooden wall in the hallway. Sharon was sleeping with her thumb in her mouth. She was dressed in a bright yellow shirt underneath a blue jumper dress with white socks and white shoes. Her curly black hair was pulled back and held by two ponytail holders. The other two children were awake, observing Paul quietly while he signed the paperwork to collect his child.

The young father recalled the first time that he gazed upon his little girl. Looking at her sleeping helped Paul to heal from a deep pain within.

Paul lifted Sharon into his arms and carried her to the car. Sharon opened her grey eyes a little bit before dozing off to close them again. Paul drove them to the beautifully preserved Gaston-Hughes subdivision where the family lived near a country club that had tennis courts, a golf club, and a community park known for its scenic tree tunnels and landscapes. Most of the homes were two story buildings with neatly trimmed lawns and gardens. The neighborhood children were scattered across the sidewalks and lawns engaged in activities of tag, red light-green light, jump rope, and much more, making it an ideal place that Paul wanted for his family.

Once home, Paul took his daughter inside their brick three-bedroom home. He loved the living room's yellow, green, and white furniture, large brown wooden record player, white lamps, wooden coffee table, brown bookshelf, color television, and off-white carpet.

Paul entered the kitchen and opened the refrigerator to find the leftover pot roast and corn bread his wife had prepared the day before. Nell usually made enough food to last a few days, leaving only the task of reheating it. Paul reheated enough for his daughter and himself, knowing his wife wouldn't be home until much later that evening. They both ate their shares of the leftovers and watched a little bit of television in the living room. Paul rested an arm around his daughter as they both lounged on the couch, thankful to be there.

Chapter 2

"Hey… I haven't heard back from you in a while. I'm just checking in to see if things are okay… Again, thanks…Jacob and I had an amazing time with you at the concert…I hope we can do more together…"

Paul lowered his head, rubbing the back of his neck. His eyes met the confused, yet hopeful brown eyes of a young woman. The woman, twenty-year-old, Cindy Spearman, had found him. She began to twist a loose strand of her blonde hair between her fingers. She wore a short red dress with white shoes, an outfit she hoped would impress him.

"I'm sorry," Cindy continued, her voice troubled. "I know you once said you weren't looking for anything serious, especially with someone who has a kid due to your past, but I didn't want to miss out on being with someone as special as you…I know it must have been a huge shock to learn about my son at the concert, and I'm truly grateful that you didn't make a big deal out of it in front of him and somehow managed to get him a ticket …I was hoping that once the truth came out, you'd change your mind…"

Cindy grabbed ahold of Paul's hand that went limp.

"I haven't," Paul confessed, pressing his lips thin, after a lengthy period of silence that grew awkward.

"I said I was sorry, okay! Why is this a big deal when it doesn't have to be? I don't understand… Kids gravitate to you, and you do an amazing job with them, including Jacob! Don't tell me that you are willing to throw everything away because things didn't work out with some woman whose been gone for years! It's time to move on! You and Jacob get along. He can be your kid, if you let him. He will be anyway, if things get more serious."

"Jacob's a good kid and I enjoyed spending time with him, but, I can't do this...I can't. How could you put all of us in this situation?"

"Um, we are dating, and I wanted to be honest because ... I'm really starting to fall for you. We can still have fun swinging, partying, and doing LSD. We're already doing it!"

"That's being honest? Up until a few days ago, I was told Jacob was some kid you babysat once in a while for extra money, not your son! I'm more confused than ever! Are there any other lies that I am unaware of? Where does Jacob stay when we're out partying all night? Don't tell me you leave him at home by himself! Cindy, please don't tell me you do LSD in front of him..."

"Stop acting like you're so innocent! Who are you to judge me? You have a kid out there somewhere and do the same things I do, but that makes me a bad parent? At least I know where my kid is! Maybe the other girl left with your kid because she knew you were crazy!"

Paul's heartbeat stopped at the moment. He gave Cindy a slow, disbelieving headshake before he hung his head. He was at his wits end.

"I-I'm sorry, Paul," Cindy began. "That didn't come out right..."

Paul tuned out the rest of what Cindy had to say. Sure, Cindy was right. What kind of father was he? What kind of father didn't know where his own kid was? He often pondered that himself, for many years, only it hurt more that someone else spoke those words. Maybe it was good that Nell had left, especially if she knew how he turned out. Paul needed a drink, to cloud the haunting, dark thoughts...but, that wouldn't change anything. Maybe some drugs...any would help... to help him forget...Paul *needed to get away before he would be tempted to return to the person that he was the first semester.*

"Where are you going, Paul?" Cindy asked.

Ignoring her, Paul continued to walk away, his eyes brimming with tears. His chest quivered, choking back a sob.

When the television program ended, Paul seized the opportunity to play catch with his daughter outside while there was still a little bit of daylight. Sometimes when the little girl would throw, she would come up short, but they would both laugh and continue. Also, they would run and chase each other on the front lawn, followed by Paul giving the child a playful tickle or a lighthearted lift. The sounds of laughter between Paul and his daughter always touched his heart in positive ways beyond what he could imagine describing. Another favorite pastime of theirs was pretending they were circus animals. They would humorously growl, curl their fingers into claws, walk on their hands and knees, and much more, gaining Paul a reputation of being a *fun dad* to the younger neighborhood kids who would occasionally join in on the fun.

After their play ended, Paul checked the mailbox to see that it was full. He took the mail and returned inside the home with his daughter. Paul began to scan the letters and envelopes with his eyes and fingers. Most were advertisements, letters from organizations seeking donations, a water bill, etc. The young man placed the mail on the kitchen counter, refocusing his attention to Sharon. It remained somewhat surreal, having the little girl with him. The *"I love you, Daddy"* told to him melted his heart regularly as well as the snuggling, shared love of music, and father- daughter moments. Sharon had a great deal of energy. She and Paul would listen, sing, and dance to the music from the records and television programs that promoted music, ending the songs with an excessive hoot and holler.

Fatigued, Paul slumped down on the white sunken couch, resting his head against the soft back pillows. His eyelids grew heavier, and his lips curled into a pleasant grin. He observed Sharon continue to sing along to the record full of children's music and play with her growing collection of stuffed animals on the floor. With a steady heartbeat and pulse, Paul closed his eyes and began to snore softly, dreaming of the generous day he had experienced.

Later that evening, Paul woke up to find himself covered in a warm and soft, orange blanket. He heard giggling from the hallway that led to Sharon's bedroom. Paul folded the blanket and placed it on the arm of the couch. He walked to the entrance of his daughter's bedroom where the door was slightly open. Inside he saw his wife curled up next to Sharon in bed with a storybook in her hand. Sharon had changed into her pink night gown. The story being read was about the lives of baby animals and their families. Soon, the story ended. Paul's wife closed the book and kissed Sharon on her temple, stating, "Goodnight, baby. Mommy loves you."

"I love you too, Mommy," Sharon stated, her eyes shifting to the door, "and I love you too, Daddy!"

Paul's wife, Nell Boudreaux, spotted Paul at the door frame. Nell Boudreaux was a twenty-two-year-old attractive woman with dark brown skin, dark brown eyes, and black hair styled in mid-length soft curls. She was wearing a patterned multicolored dress with red wedged shoes. Her white wedged shoes were placed on the floor. She shared a warm smile with her spouse.

"I love you too, babydoll," Paul said to Sharon. He almost missed it, the story time and goodnight kisses. He entered the room, kissing his daughter on the forehead.

Nell slid from the bed, grabbed her shoes, and placed the storybook on the bookshelf as Paul turned out the light. They closed the door behind themselves, leaving the little girl to have sweet dreams.

In the master bedroom, Paul wasted no time wrapping his arms around his wife as they straddled inside. Nell giggled at the soft kisses that began to caress and tickle her neck. Smirking impishly, Paul began to unbutton his wife's blouse from behind, turned on by the gentle sighs that escaped her lips.

"It's not nice to keep your husband waiting, Mrs. Boudreaux," Paul breathed, holding his wife close.

"Forgive me, bad boy," Nell laughed, turning around and giving her husband a deep affectionate smooch.

After making love, Paul rested in Nell's arms. He was dozing in and out of sleep. It was pleasant having his wife gently brush his hair with her fingertips. Paul kissed her bosom and repositioned himself to spoon her.

"So, tell me how things went today," Paul said softly.

"It's been stressful," Nell responded, "having four major tests this week, but I think I did well. Two down, two more to go! I appreciate your extra help with Sharon; she can be a handful and you have your own classes to study for also."

"Don't worry," Paul told her. "Everything's been as sound as a pound. I don't have any tests this week. The only major thing that's coming up is this group project and I'm confident that it'll go well."

"You're always so positive, Paul. But what about your reserve duties? Isn't that coming up too? I'll make sure things run smoothly, so you won't have a thing to worry about when you get home."

"Yeah, but it's usually a weekend where I go to the armory to clean the guns and other equipment. I'll be good and sweaty."

"The shower will be running as soon as you get home."

"Mmm, will you be in there waiting for me?"

"Of course!"

They both laughed. Paul began to hum a peaceful tune, closing his eyes and burying his face partially in his wife's hair.

"What song are you humming?" Nell asked.

"Nothing in particular. Just something I felt like humming because I'm happy."

"It sounds nice, maybe you can make up some words to go along with it to sing one day."

"How about now? Let me talk about my sunshine, my good ole' valentine, that good ole girl of mine… I hope she's jivin', bein' my sunshine, in my arms. That beautiful, lovely, sunshine. I like kissin' her lips and feelin' those hips. Wait, oh, oh, my sunshine, o mine, will you always be mine?"

"That sounds beautiful, Paul," Nell smiled, resting her hand on top of his and intertwining her fingers with his. She gave Paul's hand a light squeeze before bringing his hand towards her lips to kiss.

Paul took a long, cleansing breath. He thought about the box of letters sitting on the nightstand on his side of the bed. The box contained the letters his wife had written to him years ago, as the teenage girl who loved and cared about him and their relationship. Paul had already responded to several letters, occasionally leaving handwritten letters on his wife's nightstand to surprise her.

"I'm getting sleepy," Nell yawned. "Goodnight, Paul. I love you."

"I love you too, babe," Paul said kissing her shoulder. "Honey, before we sleep, I wanted to ask something."

"Sure, what is it?"

"Since things are winding down, one of my classmates invited us to go watch the football game this Saturday at his place...I'd like for you to come with me. It doesn't seem right to be invited to all these get-togethers with friends and leave you home. Aren't we supposed to be doing things differently this time? We're married and I want to share more experiences with my wife."

"I don't know, Paul... I won't feel comfortable being the only black person there..."

"Babe, we're not in Wood Oak anymore. I haven't heard these friends say one offensive word against black people the entire time I've known them. If there's anything people on my campus talk about its feminists, politics, the latest news, or drugs. I'd like for you to come with me, if even just this once. You might have a good time. You'll never know unless you give it a try."

Nell began to have an unfocused gaze, struggling for mental calmness.

Frowning, Paul waited for a response. Nell had declined to join Paul at his friends' homes for the last few occasions. Paul had accepted his wife's wishes, but still, he had hoped that one day she would change her mind.

"I promise, everything'll be fine," Paul assured her, kissing his wife's shoulder.

"Okay," Nell sighed, "I'll go with you."

Chapter 3

Am I becoming a jerk, Paul pondered, staring at the white ceiling above. The lamp on the nightstand was lit, providing a single source of light within the room that would have been in darkness without it. The young man was in his spacious apartment, with Cindy and another girl sleeping in his bed. Luckily, the night didn't lead to another disastrous incident, possibly thanks to the ultimate high that clouded everything. Paul and Cindy had gotten back together again for the fourth time, leaving him uncertain of himself, his morals, and what relationships meant to him.

Life was okay, but it could have been better. It had been exciting for a while, but Paul was not satisfied. What Cindy said a week ago made Paul wonder if some jerk was busy telling his kid how much of a loser he was for not being around. How can I when I don't know anything? How is that fair? I would have been around if I knew something! Nell, I...I guess she must have moved on by now... It's been several years and...what we had meant a lot and, I really miss...Well, no point in dwelling on the past...Nell's never coming back...I have Cindy... and whatever that other woman's name is...

Paul left the bedroom and entered the kitchen, turning on the kitchen lights. He opened the refrigerator to see that Cindy had begun to start filling it with her own favorite foods and drinks, pushing his towards the back. Not this again...Paul reached deeper into the refrigerator, removing the pitcher of water, and placing it on the counter. He opened the cabinet door, grabbing a glass and pouring the water inside to take a swig. The water soothed his throat.

Paul returned the pitcher inside the refrigerator and entered the living room. He began to examine his records near the record player, recollecting the times he listened to certain songs in the high school science lab with Nell. He remembered the small transistor radio, the dancing, the private talks, and the sincere laughter. Paul smiled, placing a record on the record player to listen to the soft music. He could imagine Nell, shy and all, nervously taking his hand as they were dancing together. She would step on his toes, but it was okay. Paul didn't mind. She was there with him. Slowly, Paul closed his eyes, seeing Nell more clearly. Her hand felt soft in his. She smelled lovely with that enchanting soft floral scent. Her lips, Paul loved how soft and full they were. Her lovely big brown eyes were as shy as ever... Nell, are you here? Have you forgiven me enough to come back? I'll make things right this time, I promise. I'll do anything to have you and our baby back...I'll be a good father, even better than my old man. How about exchanging that old school ring for a wedding ring? I bet you'd like that as much as I would. It would look swell on that pretty hand of yours. I only need a chance to make things right. Please, babe, I love you...If you love me, you'd stay...Stay forever with me... It'll be worth it in the end...

The music suddenly ceased. Cindy had stopped the record player. She stood there, unclothed, with her hands on her hips.

"Paul, it's late," she said. "Michelle and I are trying to get some sleep."

Paul's gaze flicked upward. Was the music as loud as Cindy was making it sound?

Cindy walked into the kitchen, grabbing her coat that had been placed on a chair. She wrapped it around her naked body, leaving the apartment.

Paul grumbled while he placed the record back into the jacket, adding it back to his collection.

Cindy reentered the apartment with several paintbrushes and canvases. Some were painted and some were blank. She placed them on top of the kitchen counter, leaving the apartment once more, and returning with an armful of acrylic paints. Paul was getting irritated. Cindy was beginning to add more and more of her belongings into his apartment. She had taken over the refrigerator, part of his closet, parts of the living room, and other places.

"What are you doing?" Paul demanded, entering the kitchen.

"I don't have enough room at my place," Cindy told him. "It's full of Jacob's things and my other projects."

"Why here? There's too much already! What about the studio on campus and the one you work at? I don't want that paint getting on my stuff!"

"They already have enough," Cindy told him. "If I'm going to be coming over to babysit you, I might as well leave a few more things, in case I get inspired and need my paints on hand."

Adrenaline coursing through his veins, Paul balled his fist, slamming it down on the kitchen counter. The young man was unable to take it anymore. He gave Cindy a cold look.

"I want all of your stuff gone," Paul spoke, his tone growing more impatient. "This is my apartment, not an art studio! I pay the bills and my name is on the lease. You have no right to leave your belongings here! We've discussed this before! Why don't you ever listen? Take all of your stuff out of my refrigerator, off of my counter, and out of my closet. Take them somewhere else!"

Cindy's posture stiffened, then dropped. She retrieved her items, one by one, taking them back to her parked vehicle outside.

The next morning, Cindy broke up with Paul.

Tuesday morning, Nell was at the kitchen counter browsing through the mail that had been collected the previous evening. There was a letter addressed to her from her father, causing her to take a brief pause. She held the letter in her hand but was soon distracted due to her husband's affections. Paul had approached her from behind, wrapping his arms around her waist. He began planting affectionate kisses on her neck that made Nell giggle.

"Good morning to you too, lover," Nell chuckled, resting a hand to the side of her husband's neck, and giving her body a flirtatious sway. Turning around, the loving wife gave her husband a quick smooch and wrapped her arms around him for a lingering hug.

"Mmm, good morning, sunshine," Paul said holding his wife close. "You smell nice…like bacon, eggs, and French toast."

Amused, Nell gave him a playful jab on the side.

"I am so done with you, Paul Boudreaux," Nell spoke, releasing the embrace. "Get out of here!" She placed the unopened letter down on the kitchen counter next to the other pieces of mail.

Paul went outside to retrieve the morning paper from the front lawn. He brought it back inside, placing it on the dining room table to read later. He washed his hands before assisting his wife in carrying the various plates of food into the dining room. Paul made sure that he got the plate that contained the bacon, sneaking a slice into his mouth and savoring the taste. He put two additional slices into his mouth and placed the plate next to the others in the dining room. Nell brought in a plate containing French toast. She called Sharon to the dining area.

Paul quickly grabbed the pitcher of orange juice from the kitchen, bringing it back with him into the dining room.

The family sat down and said grace. Nell began to gather samples from each plate to add to Sharon's. When she reached the bacon, her eyes squinted. She began to count softly and shot her husband a *you think you're so slick* glance.

Paul smiled away, opening the newspaper to hide the fact that he enjoyed annoying his wife. There would certainly be no more bacon for him that morning.

"I saw that Mr. Jefferson had sent a letter," Paul said. "Are you planning on writing back soon? I can drop the letter off at the mailbox on my way to the university since it'll be along the way."

"I haven't opened it yet," Nell confessed. "I don't know if I should…What could we write about without hurting the other? We barely speak on the phone as is."

"Maybe it's easier for him to write than speak about how he feels," Paul thought out loud. "Don't you want to repair things with him?"

"I don't know," Nell replied. "How? Everything that was done still hurts to this day. Why care now when he didn't back then? He probably wants to be nosey."

"Or maybe that's his way of expressing that he's sorry," Paul countered. "People make mistakes…"

"Your father didn't want to throw you away, like mine did," Nell refuted, a lump in her throat that made her tone sound on edge.

"I'm sorry," Paul said, a heaviness in his chest. "I'm sure he regrets it…"

"I don't want to talk about him anymore," Nell said, her voice flat, monotoned.

"Okay," Paul responded, taking a small bite of his French toast, and swallowing it. "Uh, I spoke to Henry over the phone the other day. He said Holiday's Garage was doing well, and things were getting serious between him and his old lady, Molly. He's waiting for the right moment to propose."

"That woman is going to have her work cut out for her, marrying someone like him," Nell muttered, taking a sip of orange juice from her glass.

"The same could be said about me," Paul snickered, lifting an eyebrow, and nodding his head.

"You're *much* more tolerable than Henry! He's as mean as a grouchy barnyard dog."

"Henry's not *that* bad," Paul told her. "He did help us out years ago and has been an extremely loyal friend…One last thing…" There was a brief pause. "Cindy wanted me to ask if you could give her a call."

"Your *ex*, Cindy," Nell stated with a sullen look. "Why are you two still speaking and what does she want?"

"Well, it's hard to avoid someone whose department is next door to mine on campus," Paul answered. "Cindy's been inviting everyone she knows to the upcoming art show that all the undergrads are having. She could be trying to be polite since we both attended her last show a while back. People on campus do a lot of networking and that's something she's good at."

"I don't trust her," Nell stated. "All those folks on that campus and she is inviting *me,* someone who isn't a student there! For all I know, she could be trying to use me to get to you. You two do have history...She's not fooling anyone!"

"In all fairness, I did offer to pay for you to attend my university, but you didn't want to go..."

"I sure won't, not after what happened at Wood Oak High School! There's no way I'm going to a predominantly white university. I'm fine with where I'm at."

Paul was uncertain of how to respond. He wished that his wife would reconsider joining him at his university, which was known to have excellent medical education. However, if Nell didn't want to go, he couldn't force her. He continued to browse the newspaper until he discovered the headline of an article that read: **Wood Oak Man Shot Dead in Hunting Accident**. Paul took a double take, his eyes eager to discover, who had died. The man who had been shot dead was his uncle, Harry Boudreaux. Harry and two other men were hunting migratory game birds when his uncle was inadvertently shot and killed. Paul recognized the name of the individual who killed his uncle, David Stanton, a man who hunted often. *How? He's always been a good shot! How could this be?*

Paul reread the article, remembering the last time he had seen his uncle alive, resulting in him giving the paper an intense stare. Paul could only imagine how his uncle's wife and children would attempt to accumulate what was left of his uncle's unwarranted assets.

"What's wrong?" Nell asked. "You look upset."

"It's nothing," Paul said, folding the newspaper. He forced a smile until Nell's facial features softened. *Maybe it is the beginning of Wood Oak becoming a better place, now that Uncle Harry is gone.*

Chapter 4

Flinging a rock into the nearby lake, Paul watched it sink into the watery depts below. He had made the best choice out of the two, but it hurt awfully bad... that damned deal...

"Who do you think you are?" Paul demanded, years ago inside his Uncle Simon's mansion. "Why'd you make those hoodlums drag me here against my will? I don't have time for this! I need to get back to Nell! She needs me!"

Simon's dull hazel eyes stared at his nephew, almost as if through him. He sat behind a stunningly crafted wooden desk in a study heavy with books and numerous documents that were thoroughly arranged. Equally well kept was Simon's tailor-made black suit with a red necktie and white handkerchief tucked in his upper left suit pocket. His greying strawberry blonde hair was neatly brushed back in a professional contour style and his pencil moustache was neatly trimmed. He calmly folded his hands before speaking in his matter of fact toned response.

"Tell me, Paul," Simon said. "Are you aware that both Wally and Harry are in the hospital with concussions along with Bill who has a severe injury to his hand? All three are threatening to identify you, Henry, and some colored girl as accomplices to the authorities for not only assault and battery, but attempted murder."

Paul's eyebrows furrowed. His mouth fell open, momentarily speechless. He rushed to his uncle's desk, slamming his hands down.

"Attempted murder," Paul gasped, a knot forming in his stomach. "That's insane! They're the ones who tried to kill us, not the other way around! Don't tell me you believe them! It's not true! Everyone, including you, knows how they are! Henry only did what he had to do to save Nell and me! That's why he shot Bill and attacked Wally and Uncle Harry. If anyone should be arrested, it should be them!"

"Would such a chivalrous heroic act matter in a parish such as Wood Oak, when there are injuries that need to be held accountable for? Perhaps you could persuade your cousins and Harry into dropping the accusations? Maybe the possible law enforcement, lawyers, notable citizens, or judge?"

Paul's chin lowered to his chest, slowly shaking his head. He felt a pulse in his throat and had a sour taste in his mouth. We're in deep trouble! What are we going to do?

"You will never see your friends again," Simon told Paul. "Their lives and yours are forever finished... unless, you do as I say... It will require a substantial amount of negotiation and compensation, something that I am certain would persuade Harry and your cousins to absolve such an unfortunate accident that took place at the Boudreaux cabin...That should be a modest cost compared to what would be in store, should you not."

Paul's heart sunk.

"I will help clean this mess," Simon continued, "only if there is... cooperation, to simply finish your education at the boys' school without further incident. This will require a halt to this...perversion for colored girls. A Dupont heir should never engage in such a distasteful manner."

Later that day on the Camellia University campus, Paul and a few classmates from his Principles of Marketing class had gathered outside of the Business School building. Professor Walton had assigned the class into teams to develop marketing strategies to increase profits for a successful business. Unfortunately, the professor assigned Ralph Mattock, a student who was failing the class miserably, as their group's imaginary Head of Marketing.

Cussing under his breath, Paul sat down on a bench while Ralph stood timidly in front of the group. Ralph was a twenty-one-year-old average-looking person with brown hair and blue eyes. He wore a blue shirt, blue jeans, and white tennis shoes. According to what Paul had heard about him, the guy came from a well-off family that had a tree farm in Florida.

"Which *type* of product are we going to market?" a twenty-two-year-old guy named Greyson Joslyn asked. He leaned against the side of the bench with his books in his hand. He had brown hair and brown eyes and wore a thin brown jacket over a green, red, and white checkered shirt, white pants, and black shoes. Like Paul, he too was a Vietnam veteran.

"I was thinking shoelaces," Ralph suggested.

"*Shoelaces?*" the rest of the group members exclaimed; their faces pinched.

"'*Why shoelaces?*" Paul asked.

"There would be less competition, and everyone uses them," Ralph said.

"There isn't a high demand for *shoelaces,*" Joel Duncan argued, scrapping his hands roughly in his curly blonde hair. His hazel eyes turned upwards. He had a brown shirt, grey pants, and white tennis shoes.

"With the right type of marketing, there *could* be," Ralph explained. "We can start a trend centered around them. All the other groups will be thinking of something easy like dresses, makeup, or food. We will stand out because our product is more challenging. Think about it, people from all walks of life use them, from the rich at the top to the poor at the bottom."

"Let's think this over," Paul said, trying to find common ground for the idea. "They are cheap and probably won't bring in much of a profit for a business. After washing them, people usually replace them after so many washes. On the other hand, they can make an old pair of tennis shoes look better and save people the cost of buying new shoes."

"Trust me, guys," Ralph said. "It is going to be a good idea; I just know it! If it's a product that everyone uses but is underestimated in our class, it's genius and profitable! Let's all meet tomorrow at the library around six to work on the project."

"Margo isn't gonna be happy about me cancelling our date," Joel groaned. "She's been pestering me for a week to see some dumb romantic comedy..."

"It's better than square dancing," Greyson yawned.

"I'd rather do that, to be honest," Joel replied. "It's actually fun."

The group members began to disperse. Paul rose from the comforts of the bench, heading down the walkway. He pondered the upcoming weekend at Joel's place. Joel had the latest color television, including a portable black and white television that he often shared with the group of friends whenever they all gathered to eat in the university's cafeteria.

Paul remembered the day the portable televisions were on sale. People had gathered in the morning to get the best deals for early customers. Greedily, there was so much pushing and shoving by customers that they broke the store's front glass window, resulting in several people being hospitalized. Paul chuckled at the thought of people doing the same for Ralph's shoelaces. He wondered if he should pitch the idea. Perhaps his other classmates would find it as humorous as he did.

There were several students gathered outside on the sidewalk that divided the business building from the art building. Paul recognized several of the art majors who were carefully assisting each other in transporting different paintings towards the downstairs Crimson Art Gallery. He greeted two of the students as they crossed paths.

Cindy exited the entrance to the main art building, a handkerchief in one hand, and her brown eyes puffy from redness. Her hair was pulled back into a single ponytail. Her brown dress was partially hidden behind a white paint-covered apron. Her white shoes were slightly worn and had old, dried remnants of paint.

"Hey, what's crackin', Cindy," Paul greeted her, stopping in his tracks. "You look a bit down."

"Hi, Paul," Cindy sniffled. "I'm fine…"

"You don't look it; Anything I can do to help?"

Cindy rubbed the back of her neck and shook her head. She released a heavy sigh.

"As you know," she told him, "I've literally been killing myself to tell everyone I can about the art show at the Crimson Gallery, including Gary, the jerk who is supposed to be my new boyfriend! You'd think he would care, but he doesn't, at all! Yesterday, I invited his friends, and all Gary could say was, 'nobody cares about that, Cindy.' I'm so upset that he would humiliate me like that in front of them! I don't think we'll be able to go over to Joel's because I'm afraid of what Gary might say in front of everyone!"

Paul gazed inward before speaking, "Don't let him get you down. Think of all the other people who are more than willing to go to the art show. You don't have to bring him along to watch the game at Joel's place. Everyone'll still have fun together, with or without him."

"Yes, but I'm his girlfriend and he should be the *first* willing to go! It's not that he's busy or anything! He lost his job two weeks ago and expects Jacob and me to move in with him. He isn't aware that I know he's behind on his bills! I hope he's not expecting *me* to pay them! I'm not supporting a man!"

Paul was astonished. Was this true about Gary? Cindy's new relationship sounded like it was on the rocks. She certainly deserved better, but that was something Paul hoped she would figure out.

"Do you think, asking him to at least support me at the art show is asking too much?" Cindy asked.

"No," Paul responded, "but hopefully, Gary will be there. It means a lot to you and if he truly cares, it should mean a lot to him too...Are things going well with Jacob?"

"Yes, he's doing very well! Thanks for mentioning him! Paul, you look better...I'm glad."

Paul smiled and began to gaze at his watch.

"I better keep on steppin'," Paul said, his eyes lighting up. "I got to head out and get my babydoll."

"Paul, before you go, is Nell going to give me a call?"

"It's up to Nell. I don't know if she'll be there for the art show. It's been a stressful and busy week for her."

"I see…Once things settle down, ask her again for me. I have a neat idea for an art series that's going to be inspired by the feminist movement. I was thinking of adding a black woman, catch my drift?"

Paul tilted his head away. *Huh? What is Cindy talking about? Since when was Nell considered a feminist?*

"When hired for jobs, women don't make nearly the same amount of money as men," Cindy explained. "We are underestimated by men who consider us weak, but we're not! Why should we stay home and depend on someone else? We can do everything men can do, if not better, and we should make a wage reflective of our skills and talents! As women, Nell and I could work together on this project to bring awareness, unity, and strength, that with numbers, women, both white and black can fight a shared oppression, the oppression brought on by these pathetic men who are too lazy to do things for themselves and get a hard-on by oppressing women!"

This is starting to become too much, Paul thought, closing his eyes quickly to escape. *All of this because of some chump? Why not work it out or dump him? Why start a campaign against all men because of the actions of one? Why involve my wife? This has nothing to do with her! She does not need to be involved in this madness.*

"Think about it, Paul," Cindy continued. "Isn't life hard enough for all women by carrying, birthing, and raising a child? Women should go further to get our points across, in a silent protest, starting with withholding sex with men."

Paul listened no further. *Over my dead body! I can't take it anymore. I can handle the strikes and protests from the phone workers, the teachers, and transit workers, but I'll be damned if any of this involves my bedroom!*

"I have to get my daughter," Paul hastily reminded Cindy as he resumed his walk towards the university's parking lot. "Bye, Cindy…Chill out…" The young man couldn't get into his vehicle fast enough, nearly dropping his keys to the ground as he dug into his pants pocket to retrieve them. He started the car, relieved to drive away.

Chapter 5

"Thanks, I'll be heading to South Carolina soon for training and will give a call back later."

Paul hung up the phone and departed the phone booth. Now eighteen-years-old and completed with the boys' school, he no longer had to adhere to his uncle's agreement, fulfilling it. His greedy Wood Oak family had been paid their dough. As costly as it was, Paul felt it was worth the hassle, if it meant that they would no longer pursue him and his friends. Now, it was time for Paul to get what he wanted for himself: the desperate reconnection to his expecting girlfriend before he would leave for training.

Paul reached into the pocket of his jacket, removing the gifted, white handkerchief that had been given to him by Nell months ago. He unraveled it, revealing the small black box inside that contained a beautifully crafted diamond ring. He hoped that it would fit her finger. It was perfect, like Nell, and beautiful in every aspect. The next time they would meet, he hoped she would be surprised to see her boyfriend pop the question. All that was left was finding her.

When they left the daycare center, Paul drove Sharon to the popular local pastry shop named Del Pastries. The shop was a brick building that was painted blue and white. The establishment usually had ten or eleven cars parked outside from parents who wanted to give their children afternoon treats. The shop had been recommended by their neighbors, the Reeves family, who frequently treated their children to cupcakes and cookies.

Sharon always had a glimpse of wonder when her father or mother brought her to the shop. It was amusing to see her go to the display area that had decorative wedding cake tops.

Not for a very long time, Paul would think with a lighthearted chuckle, observing his daughter.

Sharon's second favorite part of the store was the front center display case that showcased rows of sweets. Her weekly favorite had always been a vanilla cupcake with a tall rainbow-colored buttercream icing piled high like a twisted ice cream cone.

Often, childhood memories would flood Paul. The tiny, squared cakes, known as petit fours, were a delicacy his mother, Helen Boudreaux, served every other weekend to house guests. The Wood Oak Women of Light were composed of prominent women who planned monthly meetings at the Boudreaux home where Helen served as Hostess to the other women who had roles such as Publicity Chairman, Program Leader of the Month, etc. Most of their planned charity work focused on obtaining clothing for those in need, budgeting, gathering food or reading materials for community members, and much more.

Paul recalled his mother wearing her white wide brimmed hat and yellow sundress. Her smile was captivating and cheerful, like his. She adored petit fours, always incorporating them in her afternoon tea arrangement that also had scones, macaroons, tea, and sandwiches.

"How may I help you today, Mr. Boudreaux?" the owner, Mrs. Donaldson, asked from behind the counter.

"Two of the usual cupcakes for my babydoll," Paul answered, "one hummingbird cake for my beautiful wife, and six of the apricot jam petit fours for myself."

"Yes, sir!"

Before Mrs. Donaldson could gather the requested items, Paul motioned for a brief pause.

"Sorry, ma'am, but I will need an additional six of the petit fours."

After the items had been purchased, Paul drove with his daughter along the twisty highway that led into the heavily wooded area on the outer limits of the community. He entered through the guarded gate, driving nearly two miles further into the property, and ending the journey at the entrance of an elaborate mansion. The doors opened, revealing a middle-aged butler who was named Jules.

Paul instructed Sharon to remain inside the vehicle. He approached the butler, asking, "Jules, is Uncle Simon home?"

"Yes, sir," Jules answered, "but, unfortunately, Mr. Dupont is not seeing any visitors at the moment."

"Give him these," Paul sighed, giving the butler the small bag containing the additional petit fours.

Paul returned to his vehicle, unsure as to why his uncle had been ignoring him as of late. It appeared that the man was in the process of severing ties for personal reasons. Regardless, Paul had more important issues to attend to with his wife and daughter. Sharon was eyeing the bag of cupcakes, indicating that they needed to get home quickly.

Paul restarted the car and drove home with his little girl. Once there, Sharon was permitted to eat one of her cupcakes. It quickly began to smear across her lips and cheeks with each bite. The icing appeared on the dining table and parts of the little girl's clothes, making Paul grateful that it wasn't taking place anywhere near Wilma. The napkin given to the little girl was partially soiled with icing and cake crumbs.

Paul sat next to Sharon, popping two petit fours into his mouth, savoring the sweet, delicious taste.

Mmm, like the good ole times, Paul thought.

He contemplated getting Sharon a new tea set once she was older. The little girl already loved to pretend that she was enjoying teatime with her stuffed animals, and he wanted her to learn more about the traditions that were associated with it. Perhaps one day, she could invite friends and share what she learned, like her grandmother who learned it during her travels.

Rrriiinnnggg! Rrriiinnnggg! The phone chimed.

Paul pondered whether it was his uncle, Simon Dupont. He entered the kitchen, answering the telephone.

"Hello," Paul spoke, leaning against the kitchen counter.

"Hey, Paul," the familiar voice that wasn't his uncle's spoke. "It's Stephen Barnes. I wanted to see how you're holding up and offer my condolences. I'm sorry about what happened to your uncle during the hunting accident. I also wanted to talk to Bill, but he's far from approachable in any given situation. Will you be attending the funeral?"

"No," Paul admitted. "It's a long story, but I won't be able to."

"That was one heck of a way to die," Stephen said. "Mr. Stanton had always been good with guns, so it seems bizarre for that accident to happen. The man knows everything there is to know about guns: the year, the model, how far they could shoot—everything! There's talks of a lawsuit too, did you know that?"

"No," Paul sighed, "but I'm not surprised."

"Remember how you've said you never received a yearbook for our senior year?" Stephen asked. "I got one from our old librarian, Mrs. Walsh, since she had extras. I've been trying to get people from our senior class to sign it for a while now. Nancy's been asking for it, but I'm not crazy enough to give it to her! She's been trying to get in contact with you, but I'm not telling her a thing. I told her that I didn't want to get involved in whatever she has planned."

"Why is she trying to contact me?" Paul inquired. "Isn't she still seeing Bill?"

"She is! They're engaged, but the entire relationship is a joke. I'll give you the skinny on the situation, but don't tell anyone I said anything! Kristy's told me that Nancy has been cheating on Bill throughout their entire relationship! The woman just isn't interested in the man and has attempted to end the relationship several times, but Bill went ahead and bought her a fancy engagement ring! Then, he purchased a fancy house in the Highland subdivision, placing both their names on the deed, without even marrying her yet! That's as desperate as anyone can get! Nobody knows where he's getting all this money to do this. Isn't that side of your family broke?"

I know where he got the money, Paul thought sulking.

"Could you tell me anything on my parents' old home or Sal's?" Paul inquired.

"Your parent's home is still boarded up and hanging in there. Sal's could be better. It withstood the first few hurricanes but is in rough shape. Ms. Reynolds has been trying her best to get the contractors to repair the building, but it keeps getting vandalized."

"Yeah, she called and told me that last weekend," Paul sighed. "We're pausing the repairs for a while and will restart again in a few weeks. We can be as stubborn as the vandals."

Paul stared down at his watch.

"Well, my friend," Paul continued, "I have to get going. I will give you a call sometime next week. Thanks for everything!"

"Alright, check ya later!"

Paul ended the call. He had a slight tenseness in his muscles. He still had a telephone call to make. He took a deep, pained breath while closing his eyes. Was this really his burden to bear? It would be easy to forget. Hadn't he already done enough? Was it enough for them? For himself?

The young man used his fingers to dial the number that often distorted his thoughts. The phone began to ring, making him do a hard, obvious swallow. Hanging up crossed his mind, as it had done so many times.

"Hello?" a woman's voice spoke, making Paul's body shake with a slight tremor.

"Hi, Tracy, it's Paul…Paul Boudreaux…"

"Hi, Paul! Aint you the white boy with the dynomite smile and bright eyes? It's been a *good, long* while since I've heard from you! How are Nell and the baby doing?"

"Yes…She and I got married not too long ago…How are you and Mrs. Ann?"

"Fine! Fine! Fine! My aunt finally decided to retire. She's doing good! Now, I got somethin' to say and you're the person to answer! My aunt's been receiving all these flowers from the flower shop, and it turns out that it's been from you the entire time! They didn't know why and didn't even want to tell me it had been you, but I finally got it out of 'em and been waiting to hear back. So, my question is, *why* and *why so often?*"

Paul became unnaturally quiet. He scrunched himself in the chair and his limbs became shaky. He bent his neck, gaping at the kitchen floor. His face was now downturned. The young man took a deeply disturbed breath before focusing his gaze towards the ceiling.

"Hello?" Tracy's voice persisted. "Paul are you still there? Hello?"

I can't do this, Paul thought, his heart and mind racing, wishing he had the guts to give an immediate response. If Tracy were to know the truth in its entirety, she would have excellent reason to *hate* him, with the possibility of taking legal action against him and his family. His honest response could undoubtedly reopen a terrible wound to not only the waitress, but other members of the woman's family. *I only wanted to make something right. I know it isn't enough; nothing could ever be, but I didn't know any other way to say I'm sorry for what my family has done. I feel horrible, but I owe it to Tracy and her family to be honest, even if it is difficult on both ends. I'll just hope for the best outcome...*

"I-I'm sorry," Paul professed, his voice nearly cracking. "I truly am, for not saying anything beforehand...but my...my Uncle Harry was the person who killed Mrs. Ann's son, Otis...I'm sorry, Tracy, but I didn't know how to tell you nor Mrs. Ann when I found out you were related to him...There was nothing that I could have done to prevent his death...I was a child myself when it occurred that day..."

"What," Tracy stated, her tone shaky and disbelieving. "What are you saying, Paul? How do you know that it was *your* uncle who killed Otis?"

"Tracy, my family and I are from Wood Oak, Louisiana, the place where Otis died… I *know* it was him because I recognized Otis in a picture from Mrs. Ann's house… I used to see him sneaking into my aunt's home many times when my uncle was away. They were having an affair…"

There was a lingering silence at the other end of the phone, followed by an audible exhale that caused Paul's chin to drop to his chest. Time seemed to slow down. Feeling cold all over and nauseous, Paul expected nothing less than to have Tracy cuss him out, or make a declaration of vengeance, or end their conversation.

"This uncle of yours," Tracy commenced once more, "how's your relationship with him? Have you considered contacting the police in Wood Oak about him, to tell the truth about what happened? He needs to be brought to justice for what he's done."

"That uncle and I have *no* relationship whatsoever. If it were up to him, I'd be dead too. If it means anything, he did die recently in a hunting accident… The law enforcement in Wood Oak are no good either. They've been known to help cover up murders. My, uh, grandfather has worked with them in the past…There's an entire network…so, it wouldn't do any good. It's not that I don't want to help. If I could, I would be there and not here…I'm sorry…There's not much I can do that won't result in making things worse…"

"What was your aunt's name? The one that Otis was having the affair with…"

"Henrietta."

"Henrietta! Yep! That is Otis' old girlfriend's name! That woman is a fraud; she aint fully white either! Her grandmother is Negro, like Nell and me. Otis was engaged to Henrietta long before she left him to marry a white man who was your uncle."

What, Paul mouthed, listening intently, and shifting in his chair. *Then that means....*

"I wish we could have talked about this years ago," Tracy said, "but I can see why you wanted to keep silent...In reality, you had no control of the situation, but Otis didn't deserve to have his life taken away by anyone other than God."

Paul nodded, with relief from within.

"If it means anything," he said. "My uncle and aunt's marriage wasn't the best... I hope I didn't upset Mrs. Ann by sending the flowers. I wanted to apologize for my uncle's actions and thank her for all she's done for my wife and I... I do plan on opening several businesses in the future, with the help of a friend. I wanted parts of the proceeds to go towards Mrs. Ann. It won't replace her son, but since she had retired, I want to offer her the best retirement I can. Things are still being worked on towards building the first store, but in the meantime, I will send her a monthly allowance to do as she sees fit for the remainder of her golden years. For the last few weeks, I've been working with an attorney to draft a plan for her. He should be getting in touch with her soon."

"Wait, you can afford to do all that?"

"I can and I'm going to."

At the other end of the phone, there was a long silence.

"I-I don't know what to say...T-thank you!"

"No, thank you for giving me the courage to tell the truth. I will be giving her a call next now that you've given me the strength to do so."

Chapter 6

"Hi, my name's Paul Boudreaux. I'm searching for a woman named Nell Jefferson."

There was an extended pause at the other end of the line.

"Sorry, but nobody lives here by that name. Maybe she was the previous tenant before me...."

"Okay, sorry to bother you. Have a great evening, sir..."

Paul hung up the phone, completing the daily search for the evening. The responses were the same. No one knew who Nell was or it was the wrong person. Paul had recently returned to the United States and made aggressive efforts to continue his search, even involving a private investigator to trace Nell and her family before he left for Vietnam. All efforts resulted in dead ends. She was gone and Paul's spirit was broken.

The young man was now twenty-one years old and had enrolled himself in a southern ivy league university. He had survived Wood Oak, Vietnam, and other places deemed unsafe, only to find himself unhappy and alone. It seemed unfair. He had done what he could, taking a considerable amount of risks to do the right thing. However, it seemed all for nothing!

Paul stared into the night sky speckled with dimly lit stars. He began to laugh about the deal he made with his uncle. Nell was gone and stayed gone anyway! All gone! Maybe it was all for the best, for everyone but him. Paul began to wish he had died in Vietnam. Hurt began to surge throughout his core, turning his face red as he began to cover his face with his hands. His laughter soon became sobbing. He began to think of how stupid it was to dream and want anything. What good was it, only for it to be taken away?

Two weeks later, Paul had been invited to an off-campus party by a classmate. It was one of Dan Jones' parties, where people were known to get fried. Dan was on the brink of expulsion, but the jive turkey seemed to know more about life than anyone on campus. He knew where to get the best drugs, knew how to handle the pigs, knew how to make mulah easily, and much more. Nothing troubled him and he was the happiest bastard on campus with loads of cash and girls with jugs flocking to be at his side. The man was a smooth talker with a growing flock of university students who always seemed to follow his lead, no matter if it even put them at the risk of sharing the same fate of expulsion.

Dan was sitting on the couch passing a joint to a brunette. Next to her was a couple with their lips plastered on each other's faces. The apartment had a large number of people who were drinking, dancing, doing drugs, and barely sneaking away to do one another. Music was playing in the background that also had a thick cloud of smoke.

"You're cute. Wanna dance?"

The smoke from all the heavy smoking burned Paul's eyes. He could barely make out the person who asked. It was an attractive blonde with brown eyes. She danced to the hypnotic sound of the music playing.

"What?" Paul asked.

"Wanna dance?" the woman repeated.

"No," Paul said flatly. He eyed the exit. The smoke was hurting his eyes badly. He began to cough.

"Okay then," the woman said. "I'll get to the point. Wanna fuck?"

What?

Paul did a double take. Did the woman just ask him if he wanted to fuck her? What kind of woman was she? She had to be kidding! Instantly, Paul began to laugh, for the first time in quite a while.

"No, really, I want to," the woman repeated.

"Could I at least know your name first?" Paul laughed.

"Cindy Spearman. What's yours?"

"Paul Boudreaux."

"Okay, Paul Boudreaux, wanna fuck?"

It had been a while since Paul had sex with someone. Cindy was attractive with an offer his body was willing to take, but his heart and mind remained hesitant. What was he to do? Wait forever? He tried so many times before, only to be let down. How many more times was he to be disappointed? Paul knew absolutely nothing about Cindy other than she was there and willing. Was the woman even a good kisser or good at sex?

"Sure, we can do that," Paul answered, giving her a smirk, "but first, let's go ahead and dance. One of my favorite songs just came on and it's been a while since I danced with someone beautiful."

Equally surprised, Cindy agreed, fulfilling the request until the song had ended. Cindy was a nice dancer and Paul could see that she had nice legs. Amused, Paul kissed her, and it was pleasant.

Cool, Paul thought. I'll see what she can do. A deal is a deal.

They left the party in Paul's car. Paul went to a nearby gas station, purchasing a box of condoms. It was to be a one-time thing, and his days of letting any woman tug at his heart strings were to come to an end.

On Wednesday evening, Paul's small business group had completed their marketing strategy to attract more customers for their shoestring product. They decided to market to a younger demographic, aiming for more colors and designs that appealed to young children. The group decided to make Paul the prominent spokesperson since he had the most charisma and experience of having a child.

When the meeting in the library ended, Paul was free to leave, but he had other plans. He traveled to the other end of town where his wife, Nell, attended South Aster College. The sun began to set on the horizon and the drive was smooth, with few vehicles on the road.

The Washington-Harris subdivision was predominantly black with southern mom-and-pop restaurants, a gas station, clothing shops, and churches. There was an airport and a few primary and secondary schools within the vicinity that had a bridge that separated the highway. Behind the businesses were rows of one-story middle-income homes.

Some residents remained out and about, particularly children and teenagers who were outside playing basketball, riding their bicycles, or playing on the carports or lawns. The majority of adults sat outside on the front porches or stoops engaged in conversations, smoking, or taking a moment to go outside to call their loved ones inside for supper.

Paul drove to the small campus. There were only a few people on the property, just a few individuals making their way to what appeared to be a library parking lot and a few stragglers walking across the campus in small groups of two or three. Paul eventually stopped in front of the S.

Robinson Nursing School, one of the larger, red-bricked buildings on campus. Leaning forward, the young man rested an arm over the top of the steering wheel. He had a floating sensation within him the longer his eyes remained on the school. He envisioned Nell achieving her dream of becoming a nurse and being even more proud of her. The fruits of her labor and sacrifice would mean persevering in the end.

Paul's grey eyes darted to the American flag that fluttered in the wind near the building. If any dream was to come true, he prayed for Nell's to be fulfilled the most. When Paul returned home, he was pleased to be welcomed with the warm, loving embrace of his daughter.

"Daddy's home," Sharon spoke with excitement, her eyes and mouth beaming. "Daddy's home!"

"Hey there, babydoll," Paul stated, lifting the youngster into his arms to plant a kiss on her cheek. "Daddy's glad to see you too! Where's Mommy?"

"In the kitchen!"

"Mmm, and whatever she's cooking is making Daddy hungry!"

"I'm hungry too!"

"Let's go and see Mommy!"

They both entered the kitchen where Paul was welcomed home with a warm kiss from Nell. Paul playfully began to sing out loud, taking his wife's hand in his, leading her in a brief waltz. Nell giggled until her husband unexpectantly gave her a quick dip. Caught off guard, Nell released a surprised shriek that was followed by a laugh of relief when Paul brought her back up. She gave him a playful shove that resulted in him giving a light chuckle. "You play too much, Paul!"

"I loooovvvee you, I love you, I love my foxy momma," Paul sang.

"I *guess*, I love you too," Nell replied, smiling, and rolling her eyes. She grabbed a dish containing baked macaroni and cheese and brought it into the dining room that already had Paul's other favorites, such as meatloaf, mashed potatoes, green beans, and corn.

Paul hurried and washed his hands. If there were ever a way to a man's heart, it was his stomach and Nell knew Paul's well.

"Alright," Paul uttered sitting at the head of the table, while the rest of the family took their seats. "When did you find the time to do all this? I thought this week was busy."

"It didn't take too long to make," Nell told him. "Plus, I think *someone* deserves a treat after all the help he's been giving this week."

They exchanged smiles and began to pass the food before digging in. Paul couldn't believe how much more satisfying the food tasted that evening. Everything was meaty and cheesy, just the way he liked it, hitting all the right notes on his taste buds. Almost as if sensing her husband's ultimate appreciation, Nell shyly smiled down at her plate.

"How did things go with the group?" Nell inquired, peering at her spouse once more.

"Great," Paul stated. "We got a lot done... Mmm, this is good! We present next week but need to tweak a few words to sound more convincing. We may not fully agree on everything, but I think it forces us to think about scenarios in which we may not have full control and learn to negotiate. How about you? What's the skinny on your campus?"

"Things are fine," Nell told him, "Tomorrow the study group is coming over. We'll do our best to keep the noise down so you can study and work on your assignments… Guess what, I found out that the nursing school is getting new equipment for the labs. Everything's going to be brand new!"

"Wow, that's stellar," Paul indicated with giddiness. "I'm excited for you!"

"And *somebody else* has good news to share," Nell declared, her tone full of pride. She passed Paul an envelope that contained a folded note that he hadn't noticed on the table before.

His body posture perking up, Paul paused to examine the paper. His eyebrows furrowed and released as he began to read the handwritten note:

Mr. and Mrs. Boudreaux,

Sharon has been such a delightful help to everyone at the daycare center. She is well-behaved, sweet, and considerate to all the other children and adults. Each day, she is excited to participate in activities and is always volunteering to lend a helping hand. A few days ago, during lunch, Sharon offered half of her sandwich to Ms. Dillard who had forgotten her lunch at home and was waiting for take-out food to be delivered. I thought that was so thoughtful and amazing for someone so young to be selfless. I wanted to share this news to thank you both for having Sharon be a part of our Daycare family.

Mrs. Frazier

Paul folded the letter, putting it back into the envelope. Sharon watched her father, inquiring as to what to do next. She anxiously stuck her thumb into her mouth. Now facing his daughter, Paul beckoned his daughter towards him. Smiling, the youngster did so to receive a warm hug and kiss on the head from her father.

"I'm proud of you, babydoll," Paul said. "You're such a caring little girl. I *think* we might go to the toy store soon and pick out a new toy to join Bubba and his friends for teatime."

Paul gave his daughter a wink and the little girl gave a favorable cheer. When dinner was over, the family watched television for a few minutes, read Sharon's bedtime story, had goodnight kisses, and went to bed in their respected rooms.

"I thought about what we discussed," Nell told Paul, who was getting ready for bed. "I called my dad and we talked for a few minutes. It was awkward and didn't last long, but it's a start. He told me that he was glad I called and was in college working on my degree. He also wanted to thank you for the mail and pictures that were sent…"

"That's good," Paul said calmly. "Maybe, your folks could visit sometime. They could stay in the spare bedroom."

"Yeah, but that would be strange for us."

"Nobody needs to sneak around this time," Paul chuckled turning off the lamp's light.

The lamp 's light flicked on.
"I-I'm sorry," Paul said.

Cindy stared at him. It happened again, the night terrors that brought the sudden screams and unexpected jolts from the bed. Paul was naked on the floor. His leg began to throb from the fall and his arm was equally hurt from hitting the nightstand.

"Are you okay?" Cindy asked.

Paul brought his knees up to his chin, not saying a word. He closed his eyes.

"Yeah," he said.

"Things'll get better, Paul," Cindy told him. "Just...chill, okay."

I'm trying, Paul thought. I want to, but I can't. I think, I'm fucked...I'm fucked...

Cindy lit another joint. She got out the bed and sat down next to him on the floor. She passed the joint to Paul, who took it graciously.

"I...I think you should leave," Paul said.

"Why?"

"Aren't you scared? I...I don't want to do anything to hurt anybody, especially you. It's not safe to be around someone like me. When I'm awake, I'm fine...but when I fall asleep, I can't control myself."

"You wouldn't hurt a fly; you're just jumpy at night is all...sometimes, people get that way after trauma and want to push people away..."

Paul inhaled and exhaled the smoke. He passed the joint back to Cindy.

"People come and go," Paul sighed. "They never stick around, no matter what."

"Sounds like you were really hurt," Cindy told him.

"I was, but, oh well...Nothing matters anymore."

"I'll stick around. I think you're neat."

"Why?"

"You're good looking and know how to fuck."
They both laughed.
"That's a straightforward way of requesting for someone to stick around," Paul laughed.
"Also, you seem to be a nice guy and easy to talk to," Cindy added. "I know you're not looking for anything serious, but until then, we can be there for each other."
"Deal, I think you're cool too. You're down to Earth and creative. I like the paintings you showed at the studio. I wish I could paint as well."
"I got this job at a studio downtown. We can check it out later today, if you're up for it."
"Sure, I'd like that."

Chapter 7

Months later, it had been a few days since Paul had left the clinic. A new semester at the university had begun a week ago, and Paul was done partying. Enough was enough. He heard more and more stories about people contracting diseases and overdosing. To make matters worse, Professor Kingsley had laid everything on the table to Paul in his office. His time at the university was on the line by a thread and this new semester would determine whether he would remain. Last semester, his grades were the lowest they have ever been. Whenever Paul would take a test, he would fall asleep or walk out without any effort to complete it. Other students refused to sit anywhere near him, whispering amongst themselves that he smelled of drugs, alcohol, or vomit. One weekend, Paul was very drunk and woke up to find himself in a jail cell. Luckily, he was released with bail once he sobered up.

I can't keep going on like this, Paul thought. At this rate, I'll be dead in no time. I thought this was what I wanted, but this is as far from it! He grimaced as he cleared his throat. Dammit!

Knock! Knock!

Reluctantly, Paul answered the door to find Cindy there.

"How are you feeling?" she asked.

"Better, I guess," Paul responded as they both sat down on the couch.

"I'm sorry. I don't know how this could have happened, but thanks for telling me. I thought everyone was clean."

Folding his arms and closing his eyes, Paul pressed his head against the back pillows of the couch.

"We need to talk about us...I know things have been sporadic, but I don't think we need to keep breaking up and getting back together. You either want to be together or break up for good."

Paul sighed. Not this again! How many times must we go over this!

"I told you, I'm not trying to go steady with anyone," he reminded her.

"I know, but I don't believe that's true, not with how things are between us."

"Cindy, I—"

"Why keep breaking up when we're only going to get back together again? I'm sorry I lied about my son, but we can make this work."

"I'm done, Cindy," Paul confessed. "It's not about Jacob, you, or anybody else. I need to get my life back in order. I'm about to be expelled and I'm tired of feeling like crap every day. Ugh, my throat still hurts!"

"I can help with that," Cindy said, tucking her hair behind her ear. She began reaching down towards Paul's groin, but he grabbed her hand, pushing it away.

"Stop! I don't feel like it. Can't we ever sit down and talk anymore?"

"What should we talk about?"

"I dunno. Anything, I guess."

"Well, um, again, thanks for picking me up at the gallery after my car stopped working. I thought I'd probably have to walk home. You didn't have to work on the car, but I'm glad you did and now I don't have to worry about using the money I was saving up for Jacob's birthday for repairs..."

Yeah, Paul mouthed.

"Sometimes it seems like I'm walking on eggshells," Cindy confessed. *"I'm still not used to having someone do nice things for me without wanting something in return…For the last few months, even though things have been off and on, you've always been there when I needed someone to talk to or hang out when nobody else wanted to…But, I-I'm scared of becoming emotionally involved because I know you don't want anything serious, but the things you do…it's what I've always wanted in another person."*

"What? After all the things we've been doing? I hope not!"

"I want you to reconsider. We can go steady or close to it."

"Why can't you understand that I can't do that right now? I'm not fit to do that with anyone! I'm confused, angry, sad, and have a lot going on that I need to figure out on my own. My mistake was dragging someone else into this mess. That's why I said I can't be in a steady relationship right now!"

"I believe it is because of Jacob! I said I was sorry!"

"It's beyond Jacob! Look at me! I'm nothing short of a loser! What kind of role model would I be to any kid right now? I'm ashamed! Why would you want anything serious when I'm still trying not to use drugs or alcohol to sleep at night!"

"You don't have to be ashamed…I'll accept you for who you are. You can go ahead and propose to me right now. We both know what the answer will be."

"Excuse me?"

"I saw the ring you were hiding. You don't have to be afraid of asking."

"Have you been going through my things? Cindy, why would you do that?"

"Why is this such a big deal? Just go to the room and give me my ring already."

"Your ring? That ring wasn't meant for you!"

There was a period of awkward silence. Cindy's calm demeanor soon deteriorated. Tears welled upon her eyes.

"Then who is it for, Paul?" Cindy demanded.

"Nobody!"

"Bullshit, Paul! Who? Eileen? Ann? Michelle? Because I know you enjoyed fucking each and every last one of them!"

"Buzz off! It's not for anybody! That ring is old! I got it a long time ago for someone who I'm not even with anymore!"

"Oh! You can string me along but want to get serious with someone else! You're like all the other guys who use women for sex!"

"That's rich! All the women you named, you're the one who invited them over to join, not me!"

"You never turned any of them down, did ya? See, you pretended to be nice long enough to get what you want and then, boom, you dump someone like me to live happily ever after with someone else!"

"In your dreams! You've dumped me just as many times as I've dumped you! At least, I've been honest from the start. You, on the other hand, lie about everything under the sun! Do you even truly like men, as much as you complain about them?"

Wham!

Paul touched his cheek that turned red from the slap Cindy gave him.

"Get out of here," Paul demanded, giving her an icy stare.

"No, I won't," Cindy countered, using her fists to hit him repeatedly. "I'm tired of being used by you stupid men!"

"Stop hitting me! Shut up!"

"You shut up! You're nothing but a womanizer!"

Rising from the couch, Paul shielded himself with his arms. He went into the bedroom where Cindy continued to hit him. Paul went into the closet, locating the small black box that contained the ring. He snatched the ring out and stormed out of the apartment. He hurled the ring across the yard into the freshly cut grass.

"There," he shouted at Cindy. "It's gone! I've had it! Go find the ring and marry yourself, if you want the ring so badly."

On Thursday evening, Nell's study group gathered in the living room. Paul had completed his assignments and spent the remainder of the day playing catch with Sharon, something he and his father used to do before his untimely death. When they finished, they reentered the home to drink a thirst-quenching cup of lemonade and rest in a chair in the dining room.

"Paul," Nell's voice called from the living room, "could you come here, please?"

Guzzling down the last of his lemonade, Paul walked to the door frame that separated the kitchen from the living room, leaning against it.

"Yes, babe?" he asked.

The members of Nell's study group fixed their eyes upon him.

Darrius Sykes was a dark skinned twenty-eight-year-old man who worked as a waiter at a downtown seafood restaurant. He had dark brown eyes, and a short afro. He dressed somewhat flashy in a solid purple shirt, grey pants, a lot of jewelry and white leather shoes.

The second member of the study group was Bruce Thomas. Bruce was in his twenties, short in stature, and had brown skin and black hair in a medium afro. He always wore a brown leather jacket, grey shirt, black pants, and black shoes.

The third member of the study group was Sandra Batiste who was dark skinned with brown eyes and dark brown hair cut in a short, feathered look. She wore a multicolored, patterned floral blouse, a blue skirt, and red shoes.

"So, Paul," Darrius stated, "Word on the streets has it that you were a big shot athlete at your old high school in Louisiana!"

"Yeah," Paul said, his voice trailing while lifting an eyebrow, curious as to what direction the conversation was heading.

"Nell's been telling us you were a football quarterback and baseball captain," Darrius continued. "I used to play baseball myself. I played left field. What I'm getting at is that my sister, Joan, teaches physical education for the girls at South Aster High School down from where Nell and the rest of us go to college. This spring, she will be coaching the girls' softball team. We both know that baseball and softball are different, but I was wondering if you'd be interested in joining us to watch a few games once the season starts. I noticed from the window that you were teaching your daughter how to throw and catch. If you keep it up, she'll get better in time and might grow up to want to join a softball team one day. It'll be a great opportunity."

Tempted to say *no*, Paul was busy with limited time already, much less next semester. All eyes were on him, awaiting a response. Then, Paul thought, *yes, I will be busy, but watching a few games here and there might not hurt. I don't have to go to every game. It'll just be to support the team and see what it would be like, should Sharon be interested in the sport in the future. I'll give it a shot.*

"Sure," Paul said, "this should be interesting."

Knock! Knock!

The door opened, revealing Cindy with her lips pressed thin.

"I won't be long," Paul stated. "Just dropping this off…I hope you don't mind." He handed Cindy the wrapped gift with the words, Happy Birthday Jacob written on it along with a small white envelope.

Taking a steeling breath, Cindy leaned against the doorway before reaching to accept the gift in her hands. From what Paul could make out, there wasn't much going on that day, but maybe, later that could change, if Cindy wanted.

"I thought I mentioned Jacob's birthday once," she thought out loud.

"Yeah, it was important, wasn't it?"

"Why are you here? It's not like you should care or anything. Jacob's not your kid."

"No, but it's his special day and I just wanted to give him something. Well, it's been received, so I'll be on my way."

Paul barely made it back to his vehicle when Cindy approached him.

"What's this, Paul? Why does this envelope have money in it? I don't know how I'm supposed to interpret this."

"It's so you can give Jacob a nice party or birthday gift. He was super excited to go eat at Kid-PitZ Pizza when the concert ended. We all had a lot of fun that day. Today would be a cool time to celebrate there, huh? ...Um, and, sorry for being a world class jerk...I...I still have a lot of personal issues to work on, but let's just say that I can understand how important days like this can be."

Cindy nodded and smiled as Paul spoke, having her noticeable inward gaze. Paul recognized it, her usual sign that she wanted to be with him again, if he was only willing. Yet, as Paul had stated, he was not ready to open himself to the possibility of loving someone again. Even then, even as it was tempting to seek a lustful action, it would only continue a painful cycle of hurting both.

"Would you like to come inside?" Cindy asked. "We can have breakfast with Jacob and enjoy the rest of the day together, and if you want, tonight would also be nice." Paul could see it in her eyes that she wanted more of him: his heart, his mind, and his body...No...

"Thanks, but I can't..."

. Her smile wavering, Cindy spoke, "Okay, Paul...I...I, um...thanks for the present for Jacob and thanks for being sweet..." She gave him a kiss on the cheek before returning inside her apartment.

Paul sighed, entering his vehicle, and driving away. He wanted to tell Cindy a lot more about how fortunate she was. She knew she was Jacob's mother, when his birthday was, what his favorite songs were, and so much more. Maybe Nell was out there somewhere with their child enjoying moments like that too. Desperately, Paul wanted to be there too, to share those moments and whatever he could learn about them both. Pushing back a sob, he ended the drive at Camellia Lake. He parked the car, sat on the hood, and watched the birds float on the water. It was less lonesome having them there that day, but maybe, if he tried hard enough, he could bury his feelings, as deep as the lake, to a brighter future.

Chapter 8

Stuffing his hands into his pockets, Paul walked towards the back of the Wood Oak High School library. It was empty, except for the librarian who usually stayed in the front to check in the mountain of library books that had been returned. He thought about how annoying it must be to return each book to their specific sections scattered throughout the shelves. He was tempted to whistle, but the librarian hated any type of unnecessary noise in her book-filled kingdom.

Paul saw Nell sitting alone at the usual table with her books open and a pencil wagging in her hand, jotting down information on a piece of paper. He chuckled to himself, thinking that maybe she had plans to become a librarian herself, or even better yet, becoming a nun since he heard that her family attended church frequently.

The pencil wagging ceased when Nell noticed Paul. She looked back at her paper quickly. Smirking, Paul sat down beside her. He was curious about what was going through her mind whenever he stopped by. So far, they had brief discussions about school, life, and their families. Paul knew that he could continue with his life and so could Nell, but she remained faithfully at that one spot, and he found himself wanting to be there too.

Paul touched her free hand, bringing it down to hide beneath the table. It was warm. Nell paused, almost giving a little bit of resistance when Paul rested their hands on top of his leg.

"So, what perfume do you use?" he asked, hoping to break down another wall. "It always smells nice."

"Thanks...I don't remember the specific name, but it's from a collection of perfume samples that my mom

sometimes purchases for me, my sister, and herself from the mall."

Nell's hand was more relaxed.

"Do you plan on going to any of the football games?"

"No, I don't really understand it. I'm not really into sports...and it's not like anyone would want me there..."

"Everyone should go to at least one game! I'd like to see you there."

Paul pressed his fingers between Nells, caressing her hand with his thumb. He stopped immediately. What am I doing? Butterflies began to flutter in his stomach. Nell's eyes squinted questionably, giving him a darting glance. Paul let go of Nell's hand. He left the library, thoughts rushing through his mind to convince himself not to return.

Paul brought Sharon to a popular children's toy store after school. It was a large warehouse comparable to what one would perceive as Santa's workshop having just about everything anyone would want. There were many boxed dolls, board games, outdoor games, and much more.

"Joshua, wait," a mother called out to her young son who took off down a neighboring aisle.

"I want the Pretty Missus doll," an angry girl whined to her father who looked beyond frustrated.

"Yay," Sharon cheered, skipping towards her favorite aisle that contained the stuffed animals. She began to pet as many as she could, as if they were real and welcoming.

Paul wanted to see the latest electric games, but today wasn't about him; it was about his little girl. He trailed behind, waiting to see which toy she would choose.

Sharon rushed to the area that contained the enormous animals, including a life-sized bear.

"Wow," Sharon exclaimed, grabbing ahold of the bear's arm. "Daddy, look! He's bigger than you!"

Paul chuckled, watching Sharon wrap the toy's arm around herself as if it were giving her a huge hug.

"Daddy, he wants to hug you too," Sharon said.

Embarrassed, Paul began to wrap the animal's arm around himself. Sharon laughed happily, continuing her search down the aisle. Paul removed himself from the animal's arm, following Sharon who began to touch everything within her reach.

"Ooh, Daddy, look," Sharon exclaimed, grabbing a stuffed rabbit that had long ears. She brought the toy to Paul. "Can I have her, please, Daddy?"

"Sure," Paul said. "We can take her home, but let's see what else is in the store, okay, babydoll?"

Sharon nodded and they began to explore other parts of the store.

Paul returned to the library the next day. He kept his distance with both his hands stuffed into his pockets. The young man pondered why he continued to return. He had apologized for his past repercussions, even offering a token of friendship that had been declined. Paul was relieved that Nell didn't mention anything about what happened the day before when he accidentally confessed that he wanted her to go to one of the games. Why did he do it? Did he want her to see him as a star, as everyone else did? Well, she didn't like sports and apparently, not him either. She wouldn't even look at him in the eye and seemingly clenched in his presence. Liking her from a distance would be hard, but at least he tried.

Paul released a deep sigh. He pushed his chair back, rising to leave until he took notice that Nell had begun to reach for him. Her eyes were up and facing him, but lowered, like her hand had begun to. She lowered it to her side, as if she was ashamed, saddened, or both.

She wants me to stay, Paul pondered. Does she... like me?

Paul sunk into his chair, pushing it closer. He removed a hand from his pocket. At first, he brushed a fingertip against Nell's hand. Surprisingly, she took his hand, intertwining her fingers in his.

Paul's heart began to race.

Nell, do you like me?

Paul caressed the back of Nell's hand with his thumb and waited. Softly, Nell returned the gesture.

She does!

Paul purchased the stuffed rabbit for Sharon and drove them home. Immediately, the little girl began to introduce the rabbit to all its new friends.

"Honey," Nell said, "while you were out with Sharon, your uncle called. He wanted to say thank you for the petit fours. When did that happen?"

"Not too long ago," Paul informed her. "I had to leave them with his butler while he's been hiding out from who knows what."

"Thanks for taking Sharon out to get her new toy. Be careful, you're starting to spoil her!"

"That's what fathers do!"

Paul gave his wife a quick smooch. He took out his books and began to work on his class assignments, while Sharon began to play with her new friend. Nell finished cooking dinner and the family resumed their regular evening routines. Soon, it was time to prepare Sharon for bed. Nell had already finished drawing the bathwater in the tub. She left the bathroom, giving her husband a quick smooch and embrace.

"Thanks for putting up with me and Sharon this week," Nell said. "You've been such a big help. I don't know what I could have done without you. I love you so much."

"I love you too, sweetheart," Paul said, returning the kiss.

Nell walked into the living room where Sharon was dozing off on the couch. "C'mon, baby, let's get you into the tub."

Paul arranged his papers and books neatly on the coffee table. There wasn't much left to do. Nell made sure that Sharon had put away her toys and that the house was clean and that everyone was fed. Paul stretched out his arms and yawned. He was feeling tired. It had been a long day, yet he was as happy as he had ever been.

Rrriiinnng! Rrriiinnnggg! The phone rang, irritating him. Paul didn't feel like answering. This was the time he wanted to dedicate to his wife and daughter, but maybe it was an urgent message from a friend or family member. That was something to consider.

Yawning, Paul entered the kitchen to answer the call, "Hello?"

"Paul," the familiar voice answered. "It's Nancy…I want to talk or are you still 'too busy'?"

Chapter 9

Today, Nell's books were closed. She rested her head on the arm that leaned against the table. Opposite her, Paul did the same. They were holding hands again, exchanging nervous smiles. Paul lifted his hand, cupping Nell's chin to caress his thumb against her soft lips. He wanted to kiss them, badly, but he had already crossed enough lines.

"I, uh, have to go to practice," Paul said, clearing his throat.

He walked away, joining Coach Anderson and the other football players on the field. He wanted to bury thoughts of his actions deep within himself, never to resurface. He followed all the drills perfectly, yet he needed to do better, to forget what was happening off the field.

"Great job, Boudreaux," Coach Anderson exclaimed. "Keep it up!"

Paul needed to. Pushing his body to the limits, he ran, he tackled, and he threw. He was prepared for the game. His coach and the entire team were expecting nothing but the best and he was going to give it to them. At the end of practice, Paul showered and put on some fresh clothes. He walked to the trophy case to remind himself of his future as an athlete and hopes of becoming a high school coach and businessman.

On his way out, Paul joked with a few of his friends until it was time for the last to leave. Paul sat alone in the parking lot. All that remained were a few cars owned by the janitor and a handful of teachers. He remained in his vehicle, listening to the radio until the sun began to set.

Reluctantly, that was when Paul decided to go home. The house was his grandfather's, but he wasn't there. He hadn't been there for a while. Paul was old enough to be alone, but that didn't mean that he liked it. Most of his peers had at least someone home to greet them or be there later, but not him, regardless of the time it was. It was lonely and only reminded him that the only family member that cared for him would soon be gone. Paul had learned to take care of himself, but each day hurt more than the last.

"*Nancy*?" Paul exclaimed; his breath almost being taken away.

"Yeah, remember me," Nancy said, her voice sounding like it was almost on the verge of cracking, "and how much you lied to everyone years ago! I can't believe it! You always got on my case about being dishonest! Well, look at you, seeing *Nell* of all people behind my back!"

"What," Paul responded. "I didn't see her behind your back in high school! We had already broken up! Who gave you this number and why are you calling me about this?"

"That makes it worse," Nancy's strained voice bawled. "Why *Nell*? Why that cheap, floozy? She offered sex, didn't she? And like a fool, you took the bait! I did *everything, everything to make you happy*! And now everyone around town is saying you're married and have a kid too! I bet it's not even yours, you moron!"

"Why are you calling *me*, Nancy," Paul demanded, harshness to his voice. "Aren't you supposed to be engaged to Bill? Where is he right now? Shouldn't you be calling him to find out where he is? Why are you calling your ex-boyfriend from high school in the middle of the night? Why don't you move on, like a normal person?"

"A normal person? A normal person! Are *you* calling *me* crazy? You're the one fucking a *n*****, you son of a bitch! How much more disgusting can anyone get?"

"Shut up, Nancy!"

"No, you shut up, Paul! I thought about you more than that bitch ever had! I had an abortion! An abortion months before that skank came along, to protect us and our future...but me...I never wanted to say anything, knowing it would hurt you...but now... I don't care anymore! You never gave a damn about me! I hope that skank cheats and shows you how stupid you are!"

Paul's skin began to tingle with discomfort, resulting in light chest pain. Nancy let out a distressed cry.

"Nancy," Paul began, struggling to form words, between a sob he desperately tried to muffle, "You ...you could have...you could have told me...I never would have wanted you to get rid of the baby...I would have been there! How could you have done such a thing?"

"Yeah right," Nancy persisted, sniffling. "If that were true, you wouldn't have chosen that bitch instead! I hope your marriage fails and that you'll never be happy again!"

The phone call ended with Nancy hanging up, leaving Paul speechless and completely still. There was a sense of emotional numbness with a knot forming in his stomach. As his eyes began to brim with tears, Paul slowly lowered the phone's handset, barely missing the receiver. His eyes grew wider, almost unable to blink, haunted. Shaking, Paul began to sob unconsolably.

Chapter 10

"I heard your grandfather was in the hospital. If it's okay, we could pray for him together."

"You want to pray for my grandfather? Is this some sort of joke?"

Paul's neck bent forward before stiffening back up.

"No, there's a saying that should there be at least two or more people gathered for prayer, the lord will be there too. I'm not sure how bad things are, but it's the least I could do to help."

Reluctantly, Paul listened and waited for the ridiculous prayer to be over. It was one of the most bizarre things he had ever witnessed, on the borderline of being offensive. Nell seemed serious and evidently oblivious about the man and his history around the parish. The old man never would have allowed someone like her to ever pray for him, yet she was doing so willingly! Was she being sly and making fun of the situation?

"He never would have wanted anything from you, not even a prayer," Paul told her, his face reddening.

"Well, when I overheard your friends talking about how sad it was for you to go to the hospital, I figured it may at the very least mean something to you, if not him."

His upper lip curled, Paul left the library. Who did Nell think she was fooling? What made her believe she was a saint and that anyone needed her prayers?

Paul returned home once practice was over. He didn't have any homework to do, and it would be a good time to have fun at the skating rink or catch a movie. Anything to distract him would suffice. Paul picked up the phone and dialed Nancy's number.

"Hello?"

"Hey, Nance, wanna catch a movie tonight?"

"No, I'm tired."

"Oh... it...it would mean a lot if we could...I mean...I found out my grandfather's cancer has spread and gotten much worse...I...I just need somebody to help me get my mind off things..."

"We can tomorrow. I have a lot on my plate as well. Chrissy broke her leg and now I must rethink our entire routine for the upcoming game. That's important too. Your grandfather's old and old people are always sick. It's no big deal. Stop acting like a big baby."

Scrunching his face, Paul hung up the phone. He walked outside, spotting the vehicle his grandfather had given to him on his birthday. Paul climbed on top of the car's hood, resting his body against it. He tucked an arm behind his head and stared into the night sky that was clear with a few stars. Using his fingers, he pointed out the different constellations that he could remember from the time he was younger that was taught to him. Then, curling his hand, he began to remember the prayer he once thought was silly, almost offensive.

I guess, I needed it more than I thought.

The following day, Paul entered the library to see Nell sitting at the usual back table alone. He sat next to her. His hands were stuffed into his pockets.

"I don't want to talk," he said. "I'll just sit..."

Nell didn't say anything while sitting with him. Paul hunched over the table, drooping his shoulders. He pushed back a muffled sob. He figured she would make fun of him, walk away, or tell the entire school. At that point, he did not care anymore. Paul forcefully swallowed another sob.

Using the hand she always held in his, Nell began to rub his back, eventually leaning forward to embrace him.

"Daddy," Sharon's voice called out as the sound of the front door opening and closing rang throughout the home, along with the sound of feet running. "Daddy, where are you? It's time for goodnight kisses!"

Paul stared blankly into the night sky; his vision was blurred from puffy eyes. His posture was slumped on the back porch swing while he wiped his tear-soaked face with the palm of his hand. For the first time, he couldn't bring himself to respond. Tilting his head back, Paul covered his eyes with the palms of his hands, wiping the tears away and fighting back the urge to release a muffled cry. Lowering his head back down, the young man's chest quivered. Each intake of air seemed to choke him down.

The door to the back porch swung open. Playfully, Sharon's hand gripped the door handle, allowing her to swing her body forward. She was dressed in her purple pajamas with her feet bare. Her curly hair was still slightly damp from her bath. Spotting her distraught father, the little girl's sleepy, yet cheerful smile began to quickly fade into a downturned frown.

"Daddy?" the little girl spoke, her tone much lower than normal. As if her feet were frozen to the floor, she stood there. "Daddy?"

"Sharon, no running in the house," Nell's voice called out from the inside of the home. She approached the little girl with a stern gaze until she noticed that her husband was visibly upset near the doorway.

Clutching her mother's dress, Sharon tugged and buried her tearful face into her mother's dress.

"Mommy, Daddy's mad at me," the little girl wept, her voice choking.

"What?" Nell asked, glancing between father and daughter. "What happened?"

Neither Paul nor Sharon answered. Kneeling a little bit, Nell faced the little girl before saying, "Baby, Mommy is going to talk to Daddy and find out what happened, okay. Be a good girl and go back inside where Bubba is. Mommy and Daddy will be there soon to have story time and goodnight kisses."

Almost stomping from one foot to the other, Sharon began to protest, "Nnnoooo! Daddy is mad at me."

"I'm sure Daddy is not mad at you," Nell reassured the little girl who was now beginning to shake.

"Daddy is not mad at you," Paul said, finally able to push away another sob enough to regain his composure.

Calming down slightly, Sharon rushed to Paul, climbing herself into his lap, resting her head against his chest. As much as Paul wanted to be alone, he struggled to bury his emotions inside. If not, how could he explain things to her? She was a little girl who was too young to become aware of such things.

"Daddy is not mad at you," Paul repeated, kissing his daughter's forehead. "Daddy had a little boo boo outside is all. It's all better now."

Nell sat down beside Paul as he began to rock the little girl back and forth.

"Remember when you had a boo boo a few days ago?" Paul asked, forcing a small chuckle.

Sharon nodded, wrapping an arm around him, and closing her eyes.

"Mommy and Daddy kissed it and made it all feel better. Sometimes, Daddy gets boo boos too and he had a really big one tonight...but he's okay now...now that Mommy and you are here..."

Sharon stuck her thumb in her mouth, nuzzling close to her father. Nell touched Paul's shoulder, but he didn't dare look her way, worried she would inquire further.

So much for story time, Paul thought while holding their daughter.

"Maybe we can have story time outside tonight," Nell suggested, beginning a story that told about a family finding happiness within each other through difficult times. There were funny moments when Paul knew she would use certain words to make Sharon better understand. Yet, in a way, it also seemed to cheer Paul a little, as meek as the story was.

When Sharon fell asleep, the family continued to remain outside. Paul began to nod off when Nell started to speak.

"Is everything okay, Paul," she inquired.

With a pinched smile, Paul nodded. He rose from the bench to enter the home with Nell following behind him. Paul placed Sharon into her bed, giving her a goodnight kiss. Nell did the same and the couple returned to their own bedroom. Once inside with the door closed, Nell grew still watching her husband's shoulders slump.

"You and Sharon deserve so much better," Paul said, his voice audibly stressed while sitting on the edge of the bed with his head hanging low to his chest.

"What are you talking about?" Nell inquired, sitting at his side, wrapping an arm around him, and giving him a gentle squeeze.

Paul continued to be silent, slowly shaking his head.

"Paul, what is going on?" Nell persisted, tilting her head. "Everything was fine earlier. Was it the phone call?

Did something happen to your uncle or one of your friends…? Paul…?"

"It was Nancy," Paul confessed, scowling with an ugly twist to his mouth as he spoke her name. He locked his hands into a fist. "That—" The young man stopped himself momentarily to release a muffled groan as the adrenaline rushed through his veins. "She got ahold of our number somehow, called, and had a lot of things to say…"

"What did she have to say," Nell asked, her face giving a hard expression upon hearing Nancy's name.

"A lot…One of them being that she hid a pregnancy from me…and terminating it without letting me know anything until now! …God…I could kill her for what she's done!" He swung a fist into the air before slamming it down on his thigh.

"She could be lying and said those things to hurt you," Nell spoke.

"Yeah, but what if it's all true? How will I ever know? All the times she and I had sex, not once was there any word or indication that she was! It hurts…my parents had so many miscarriages and, now, it seems like I've had one of my own…How could she…? I wasn't even given a chance to help…"

Paul slightly turned his body away, hunching his shoulders. Moving closer, Nell kissed his back before resting her head against it to embrace him.

"I'm sorry, Paul," she said. "Nobody, especially you, deserved for that to have happened, and I'm sorry that you had to find out in an insensitive, impersonal way…"

"I'm a terrible father. What good is a man who can't be there for his children? I lost one and wasn't there for Sharon during the first few years of her life. I'll never forgive myself for as long as I live."

"You are not a terrible father. Stop blaming yourself for actions you had no control over. What matters the most is that you would have been there for both children; I'm certain of it! Paul, I'm so, so sorry for the loss, and Sharon and I will be here to help you heal for however long it takes. We both love you so much."

Paul could feel the gentle touch of his wife's fingers trailing his back, giving a bit of comfort.

"I love the both of you too," Paul uttered, shifting his position to hold his wife, letting their embrace linger.

Chapter 11

"I'm so sorry to hear about your grandfather, Paul," Mrs. Perkins stated. "We all are."

"You have our complete support," Mr. Perkins added. The man and his wife were almost laughable. Their marriage was on the rocks and little did they know that Paul was aware of it. Mr. and Mrs. Perkins were a middle-income, yet typical 'Keeping Up with the Jones' type of family. Whatever was the latest, they had to have, including the new family car and planned family vacation to Europe. Mr. Perkins was increasingly getting into more debt, even borrowing money from Paul's grandfather with an increasing outstanding balance. It was not surprising that they were obviously trying to weasel their way out of debt through their daughter.

"Thanks," Paul said, taking a small bite of the pasta salad Nancy had prepared.

Whenever Paul would visit, Mrs. Perkins was adamant about her daughter preparing the food and bragging about the potential notion that Nancy would be a great future spouse for him.

"What do you think of the pasta salad, Paul," Mrs. Perkins asked.

"It's pretty good," Paul answered.

Mrs. Perkins breathed a sigh of relief.

"Nancy is such a sweet and considerate girlfriend, isn't she," Mrs. Perkins stated, exchanging a smile with her daughter who sat across the table opposite Paul.

"How long has it been since they started dating?" Mr. Perkins laughed. "Going on two years! It should be getting serious soon with graduation around the corner.

Isn't it amazing how our little girl grew up to become the girlfriend of such a promising young man?"

"Helen would be ecstatic," Mrs. Perkins added. "Nancy's always admired everything about her, especially her jewelry. I remember those beautiful hats Helen would wear. Andrew made certain that she had the latest of everything. Oh, they had a beautiful marriage."

"I hope you have plans to do something with their old house," Mr. Perkins told Paul. "A nice home like that never should have been boarded up. It was the best house in town, and everyone liked going there. It needs to be used as it was intended, for a growing family."

A growing family? I know I will turn eighteen in a few months, but aren't they rushing things? I don't even know what I want! I like someone, a lot, but I don't know if that relationship is even a possibility! And I'm not sure about kids. Can I even give someone a kid when my parents struggled to have me? Everyone keeps pointing to Nancy as a good spouse, but I don't think she would make the right one for me...

The next day, Paul visited the library to meet Nell again. This time, Nell was doubtful, asking him what he wanted. He asked her if she was willing to be his girlfriend. Nell stated that she would, thus ending Paul's relationship with Nancy.

"A normal person? A normal person! Are you calling me crazy? You're the one fucking a n****, you son of a bitch! How much more disgusting can anyone get?"

Nancy's words repeated in Paul's thoughts. He scoffed, *as if she's the one to talk. At least I know who and what my wife is. It would be so easy to reach out back to Nancy exposing her to Aunt Henrietta's secret, knowing how much it would destroy her. But, why say a thing at all at this moment in time? Her knowing much later into her joke of a marriage would be even greater revenge! It would serve her right.*

Paul looked down at his breakfast plate, digging into the pancakes Nell had provided. She was being extra careful and nice to him. Earlier when he had gotten out of the shower, Paul overheard his wife talking to Sharon about being "an extra good girl." It was a nice gesture, but seemed to have made things more awkward in a way that was unusual with the level of quiet.

Once breakfast had been eaten and everyone was ready to depart for their destinations, Paul began to wonder how things could have gone had things ended differently. Could he have been allowed to raise the other child on his own? Would Nell have given him the time of day? So many possibilities, yet he was grateful that Nell was being supportive and patient with him in her own way, like she had been years ago when his grandfather, Abraham, had passed. *I wish people around me would stop dying...How many more times does this need to happen?*

"I love you," Nell told him, planting a warm kiss upon his lips. "Don't allow her to steal your joy."

"I won't," Paul promised returning the smooch, almost hungrily. His tension began to sooth as they embraced. "I love you too."

Paul released his wife and told his daughter that he also loved her, meaning every word, giving her a loving hug before turning her back over to Nell. He watched as they went into Nell's vehicle to leave for the day. Soon, he too departed from the home to the Camellia University campus to partake in his classes for the day.

Paul longed to get Nancy and her bothersome confession from his mind, but it continued to haunt him, painstakingly forcing him to have the inability to focus on his classes. Each professor's words seemed to be clearly heard in the beginning, but seemed to fade into nothingness, including the classroom, and its other students. If that was one secret Nancy had hidden, were there more? Would they be much worse than the last?

"Hey, Paul, you heard about that pot bust down in Jones County?" Greyson asked Paul, sitting down in a chair next to him after Professor Kingsley's class had ended.

"Huh?" Paul asked, escaping from the void of his mind.

"Twenty thousand plants," Greyson gasped, "all hidden in a cornfield! Imagine how much bread someone could have made! Did you know anything about it?"

"How would I?" Paul countered. "I only had some every now and then from Cindy or Dan a long time ago. I haven't touched the stuff in a while."

"Good thing, huh? At least ten people from our campus were arrested with ties to them. Cindy's name wasn't in the newspaper, but she and Dan better hope nobody rats them out to save their own skin!"

Or mine either, Paul thought, regretting that first semester the more he thought about it. *How many more damn things need to happen this week?*

"Each day there are more articles about the president's impeachment," Greyson continued. "They say he won't resign despite what people are telling him...Oh, remember that singer that everyone thought died from choking on a sandwich? Well, now they think it's because she was too fat and had a heart attack. I know I shouldn't talk, but I'd never go down like that."

Stiffness in his neck, Paul focused his gaze on the classroom doorway. He did not want to hear any additional bad news, wanting to be alone to figure out how to handle his own with the strong possibility of doing such a task another day. *Things were going well until that phone call! What's going on with my life? It seems like I'm going backwards.*

"Sorry, buddy, but I got to go," Paul interrupted his friend. "I need to clear my mind over a few things. I'll see you at Joel's tomorrow."

Off guard, Greyson responded, "Oh, okay. See you then."

Exiting the room, Paul walked down the hallway spotting a few girls sharing a newspaper and discussing their daily horoscopes. A couple walked past him, chatting about an upcoming popular television program.

Maybe writing a letter to 'Dear Mary' was an option. There were always people writing to the woman about what to do to help them solve their issues, but with so many things going on at once, which could Paul possibly write about? What fake name could he come up with? Paul chuckled at the idea of writing to the woman under Nancy's name, pinpointing the finger to her in an upturned confessional way. Afterall, Nancy and her friends did like to read articles like those back in high school, so surely, she would be shocked to read a confessional under her own name. To add fuel to the fire, Paul could inform those from high school that he kept in contact with to keep an eye on the article, thus destroying Nancy's reputation within the Wood Oak community.

Paul debated within himself should he call Nancy's old number to reach someone to give him her number so he could call her, like she did him. Only he would want her mad enough to confess more. Yeah, the more the merrier so he could use that to eventually hurt the bitch. In fact, he could call Brenda Miller who was more than likely waiting to seek revenge after their fight over him years ago.

"Hey, Paul," Cindy called, approaching him from what seemed to be out of nowhere.

God no, Paul thought, clenching his teeth with a quickened pulse. *I don't need this right now!* The last thing he wanted to hear was another ridiculous man-hating speech from a woman, especially another ex-girlfriend. *'Dear Mary,' how do I get rid of her for good?*

"You're coming to the art show tonight, right?" Cindy asked. She seemed more cheerful than before, possibly indicating that she and Gary had resolved their differences. Even though she had the scent of a sweetened perfume, it had notes of pot in the mix.

"I don't know," Paul confessed, scraping a hand over his face. "I'm not exactly having the best week. I should go home."

"Please come, I need you," Cindy begged before taking a step back as if taking a moment to study him. "You look upset. Is there anything I can do? Have you and Nell gotten into an argument? Is she upset because I invited you both to go to the show?"

"No, it's nothing like that at all," Paul said, running his fingers through his hair. "I just need some time alone. I have a lot to process right now."

Her shoulders beginning to slump, Cindy nodded. They were back to their usual pattern, him blowing her off.

As much as Paul wanted to put on a happy face, pretending that things were fine, he couldn't do it anymore. Not today, nor back then either seemed to work, as if they were destined to keep the same pattern going on.

"Okay, see you later, Paul," she said, her voice lower than before. "I hope things work out."

*Sorry, Cindy, but I can't, not tonight...*Paul went to his car, drove to the daycare, and picked up Sharon. His eyes lit up a bit upon viewing how bubbly his daughter was with her wide smile, eager to hold his hand, and skipping along the way back to the car. Before the little girl had a chance to climb in, Paul lowered himself to provide her with a lasting hug.

"I love you, babydoll," Paul said taking in a deep, cleansing breath.

She is safe, he thought over and over to himself. Nobody's going to take her away from me ever again.

"I love you too, Daddy," the little girl replied, wrapping her arms around him.

Paul kissed the top of Sharon's head. His sour mood dissipating, his face turned upwards. He closed the passenger door and entered the car to sit in the driver's seat. He turned on the car radio to be thrilled to hear a playful tune that his daughter began to sing along to. This was one of Paul's favorite times of the day, spending some alone time with Sharon. He began to sing along with her throughout the drive.

His tensions melting away, Paul ended the drive in front of their home. He helped Sharon out of the vehicle and they both entered the house.

"Daddy, I'm thirsty," Sharon squealed.

"Daddy's gonna get us some milk, okay," Paul said opening the refrigerator and pulling out the milk.

He got two glass cups and poured milk into both. He collected two plastic straws, handing one to his daughter before sitting down next to her. Grinning, Paul put his straw into the cup of milk, blowing into the drink. Immediately bubbles began to form in the milk. Sharon began to do the same, giggling between each blow.

His mood refreshed, Paul drank the last bit of milk from his glass. He waited for Sharon to finish hers and began to clean up, including washing their cups. Times like that gave him a sense of DeJa'Vu, remembering the times of his youth when he would return home from school to be welcomed home by his mother, Helen Boudreaux. Paul could remember hearing music on the radio and his mother opening her arms wide to greet him with her warm smile. If there was one thing Paul was eager to do, it was to always make sure that his little girl never became a latchkey kid, as he had become. Years ago, when Paul had moved into his grandfather's home, he was often left alone due to the elder working so much at the family store or his growing loan business. Paul would occasionally visit Henry's house, even though it was several blocks away. Henry often complained about having so many siblings, but Paul thought his friend was lucky. At least he would never be alone.

"Abe," one of the neighbors spoke one day, "I know you've been ferociously independent since Alice passed, but don't you think you need help around the house?"

"No, I don't," Abraham answered. "Nobody is going to weasel themselves into my home and steal everything I've earned."

"What about Paul? Shouldn't the lad —"

*"Get out of here, Fred. Can't you see that I'm busy? I have better things to do without you and that retarded wife of yours telling me how to run my own home." The elder shut the door in the man's face, then headed into the living room where Paul was seated studying. Abraham began a series of coughs that concerned even Paul, but knew it was better to keep his concerns to himself. "I'm heading out to the store. A n***** thinks he can waltz around our part of town and look one of our women in the eye. I'll blow his eyes right out of their sockets!"*

His feet heavy, Abraham grabbed his rifle that rested on the coffee table. He stuffed a few bullets into his pocket and made his way out the home. Paul waited until his grandfather had shut the door before running to look out the window to see his uncle Harry and a few other men waiting outside, angry and talking amongst themselves.

"Daddy, let's play with Bubba," Sharon said, running deep within the home to gather her precious toy.

Paul waited until she returned to see that she not only had Bubba, the stuffed toy bear, but Zaza the stuffed rabbit. Sharon approached her father, handing him Zaza, and rushing to the sofa to pretend that Bubba was jumping. Her eyes were full of life and joy, but it made Paul wonder, *what if during some point in time, another parent felt the same way, like the parents of the man whose life was taken away by his grandfather.*

"I'm back," Nell's voice called out from the kitchen, snapping Paul back from his thoughts.

Paul could hear the door closing shut and the sound of keys being placed on the kitchen counter. Paul told Sharon that he would return in a few minutes, leaving the rabbit on the sofa. He entered the kitchen, giving his wife an affectionate kiss.

"I wanted to talk about something that's been bothering me," Paul confessed to his wife. "I'm aware that I've made terrible decisions in the past, but also a few good ones along the way… Nell, I know we both agreed to put off having more kids for now, but, later when we are both finished with school…would you ever want to have more together? I don't mean to sound selfish, but I do."

"I'm not ready, Paul," Nell confessed, frowning. "I don't think I will be for a while…I'd like to finish school and see how we can grow in our careers. If we had another baby, it would put off--."

"Nell, you don't have to work," Paul interrupted. "You can spend time at home relaxing and doing whatever you want."

"Not with a new baby!"

"We can hire someone, anyone you want."

"Paul, I've already done that, and it was hurtful to leave Sharon with someone else while she was still a baby. Yes, I was there for the first few years, but I had to have somebody else tell me her first word, rock her to sleep when I was away, and other things. I had no choice because I had to work. I just want to finish school and help raise the daughter we already have. Another baby would be too much with all that is going on now."

"If you become a nurse, the answer is no, huh?"

"No, its—"

"Then what is it? Do you want more or not?"

Paul's face reddened. He began to feel lightheaded. Nell touched his arm.

"Just give me more time to think about it...Aren't we both busy with school and one child as is? What if you get so consumed in your own career that you change your mind later? Can't we both finish one thing at a time? As of now, having more kids is still on the table, but later..."

Tenseness in his stomach, Paul asked, "So, the answer is maybe...unless someone changes their mind...I won't...but if you decide not to, there won't be any hiding that from me, right?"

"I won't hide anything."

Nell sat down next to Paul in the dining room, bringing her chair close to his. She rested her head against his shoulder.

"I just need more time," she told him. "I thought about what you said...regarding my dad...I wasn't sure about writing him back...I thought that one or two phone calls would be enough, but afterwards, it didn't seem to be...I started to think about a response but couldn't come up with much to say without feeling hurt. I don't know... Should I pretend as though nothing happened? It feels dumb not knowing what to do. I know *how* to write, but how, to him? It's horrible, aint it? To be this way..."

"Begin one word at a time," Paul suggested, his voice soft. "Write what you would like to say, regardless of what it is. If you don't want to send it to him, you can always start over until it's something you'd be comfortable sending, but whatever you send, be honest, regretting nothing..."

"Do you regret talking to me about having more kids?"

"No, it was honest."

"If I would have said no, would there be regrets?"

"Maybe at the time, but, like I said, it was honest and—"

"I would, Paul, just not for a while… Does it change things?"

"No, babe. I still love you the same as before."

"I love you too."

Chapter 12

Gleefully, Paul danced to the song playing on the transistor radio. Giggling and swaying her legs on top of the teacher's desk, Nell watched him.

"C'mon," Paul laughed, "it'll be more fun if we both danced."

"No way," Nell laughed.

"That's not what your legs are saying!"

"Nice try; they don't talk!"

"Moving is talking!"

They were officially dating and were secretly meeting in the science lab in the mornings. Bursting with energy, Paul strutted towards Nell, singing along to the song. Tossing her head back, Nell sighed with a wide smile. She pushed herself away from the desk and Paul took her hands while swinging his shoulders and legs to the beat of the music. Nell was not as great of a dancer as Paul was, but he did not care. He enjoyed spending more time with Nell and seeing her increasingly break out of her shell.

Soon, the bell would chime, starting a new day at school.

"Well, babe," Paul said, using the new nickname given to her, "I'll see you later in class." Smiling, he affectionately kissed her, positive for more to come.

Paul was in better spirits after dinner, relieved to have spoken to his wife and learned that she had finished her exams, allowing more time to spend together. Feeling energized, the young man began looking through the newspaper to see which movies were showing at the theaters, but those listed had already begun.

Paul noticed an advertisement for the Dupont Bank and Trust that they had received yet another billion dollars' worth of assets and were expecting more. *Uncle Simon must be pleased.*

"Found anything yet?" Nell asked, sitting next him.

"Not yet. This one movie that sounded cool isn't showing anymore tonight. The shopping center is closing soon, and we both aren't feeling up for the roller rink...The only other thing I can think of that would still be open would be the art show on campus."

"Isn't that Cindy's show?"

"Yeah, but we can do something else."

"Such as?"

"I don't know. Everyone I know is either at home studying, at the art show, or on their own individual dates."

"We can go to the art show, since there isn't anything else to do."

"Really? Okay, we can take a ride on campus."

After obtaining a reliable, last-minute babysitter, the Boudreauxs took a ride to the Camellia University campus. It would be Nell's first time there, which made Paul excited. He was eager to show her as much of the campus as he could, wishing they could have taken an earlier stroll together in the morning. Nighttime was fine, but chances were high that they wouldn't have their top pick in parking. Paul drove near the gallery, observing that most of the closer spots were filled. He parked as close as he could two buildings away. What Cindy and the others did to attract guests was evidently a success.

The Crimson Gallery had many guests gathering around the entrance with refreshments and engaging in conversations. Paul was familiar with most of the art students and began introducing them to his wife. They all began discussing the paintings, sculptures, or photographs. Other conversations centered on topics such as the championship rodeo, the latest cars, which stores had the best deals, and television programs. Most artists were hoping to interest patrons into investing in promising artwork.

"Need anything to drink, babe?" Paul asked his wife.

"No, no thank you," Nell responded, looking at the different art pieces and squeezing past other guests to follow her husband.

After doing a walkaround, Paul was eager to leave. He wanted to show his wife more of the campus, such as the magnificent clock tower, the business building where he studied, the lake, and much more. He wasn't much of an art fan, and neither was Nell, but he hoped to say a few polite words to Cindy but couldn't find her amongst the attendees. *Maybe she's running late or had an errand to attend.*

Paul glanced at his watch before asking a few art students if they had seen Cindy. No one had seen her all night.

"Babe," Paul said, "you don't mind if I call and check on Cindy? She usually isn't late for her shows."

"No, go ahead," Nell said, her tone somewhat flat. She followed Paul to the outside of the phone booth, watching him enter.

Paul gathered some change from his pocket to insert into the coin slot. He lifted and pressed the handset between his ear and shoulder, dialed Cindy's phone number, and waited. *It must be something serious. It could be her son or maybe that jerk she's been seeing lately did something...*

"Hello?" Cindy's voice answered, monotoned.

"Hey, Cindy, it's Paul. Is everything alright? I was hoping to see you here at the art show. I'm here with Nell."

"Thanks, Paul, but I'm not going...Nobody cares if I do or don't."

"Really? What about all the hard work you put into your art and getting people to come?"

"Yeah, my professors think my paintings are nothing more than another cliché and average at best. I worked so hard, and people tell me they look great, but when I ask for complete honesty, they say something else...I guess I'm just average. A true artist is unique, set aside from everyone else. I'm disappointed in myself."

"I'm sorry, Cindy..."

"It's...it's not only the art show that's got me down... Gary broke up with me too an hour before the show started... and I just want to be alone. I'm sorry, Paul...I didn't think you'd come...but it's good to know that you did, and that someone showed up for me."

"I get it; I was feeling down earlier myself," Paul confessed. "Maybe we can talk another time when you're feeling better? Nell and I enjoyed viewing your paintings. Cliché or not, I'm certain most people find them to be relatable topics of discussion. The one called *Sad Lady Blues* was very expressive and my favorite one. I like the use of the various blue colors, brush strokes, and facial expressions given to each figure within. I'm looking forward to seeing what you have planned next as you discover new things about yourself and how you are able to persevere with your new work."

"Thanks, Paul…"

"Thank you too, for inviting Nell and me. Don't be so hard on yourself and keep growing with each experience. I'll check on you later to see how you are doing, okay? Take care."

The call ended and Paul departed the booth to rejoin Nell.

"So, what happened to Cindy?" Nell inquired.

"She's going through a lot and couldn't be here tonight, unfortunately," Paul answered. "I'll check up on her Monday to see if things have gotten better for her. This week's been pretty much hard on everyone…"

"It sounds like you care an awful lot about Cindy."

"It's not like that at all! She's just a friend—"

"An *ex-girlfriend*."

"That you met and understands that I am with my wife that I love very much."

Paul wrapped an arm around Nell.

"How about we take a nice walk next door to the business building and afterwards, see the rest of the campus? I'll give you the grand tour, all exclusive!"

"I'd like that," Nell beamed as Paul led the way to the next building.

Chapter 13

Saturday morning, Paul was happy to take his family to the Azalea Mall to shop and have fun. The mall had numerous teenagers, young adults, and families scattered throughout the various stores. Some teenagers were browsing the clothing stores, trying on makeup at the makeup counters, flirting, or eating food at the food court. The other adults were either walking around with their children carrying bags, window shopping, browsing the clothing from the clothing racks, or giving their children money to get a treat from the gumball machines.

Paul headed straight to the popular record store, as he did most weekends, searching for the latest song. Upon entering the store, he was greeted by a staff member named Brian from behind the register. Charles, another employee, greeted Paul while assisting a woman who was in search of a record that had a specific song.

Paul loved using his fingers to browse through the different sections that had his favorite musicians, especially to see if they had new songs or covers that had hologram vinyls, bright colors, designs, or poses displayed by the artists. His favorite musical genres included rock and roll, rhythm and blues, and disco.

"Going to the rodeo this weekend, Paul?" Charles asked when he finished tending to his latest customer.

"Nah," Paul answered, "the wife and I will be heading over to Joel's to watch the game later today and I will be visiting one of my uncles. How's business been lately?"

"Busy! Everyone's been trying to get their hands on that new hologram that you purchased a while back. Then people have been asking for new orders of blacklight posters. Those never stay long here."

"Can you blame them? Hologram vinyls are so cool. I like tilting them and seeing the images! I'm still hoping to find more to add to my collection. What do you have planned once your shift ends?"

"I dunno, might head out and play a game of pool. I have next weekend off, so I'll be joining everyone at Bobby's."

"Cool. Hey, is it true that there's a penny shortage going around?"

"Maybe, but not here, at least not now. I read that some places might replace the penny with paper scripts, stamps, or simply might round off the price."

"In what capacity?"

"Like if an item costs, $2.51, they might charge $2.50 instead. If you have any wheat-back pennies, I'll be more than glad to take them off your hands."

"Thanks, but I'm looking to collect a few myself!"

Both men continued to talk until Charles had to tend to another customer. Paul gathered the records he wished to purchase that day, paying for them at the register. He, then, went to the women's and children's clothing store that he knew Nell and Sharon would be. The young father soon spotted them in the children's section where Nell had an armful of clothes. Sharon stood at her mother's side whining. Paul lifted Sharon into his arms and kissed his wife.

"Got everything?" he asked.

"I can't decide on if I should get her the plaid jumper or the denim jumper."

"Why not both?"

"I don't want to spend too much—"

"I have more money if needed."

"It's okay. I'm trying to stay within budget."

"Let's switch," Paul spoke exchanging his daughter with his wife for the clothes.

"Paul," Nell began, but Paul headed to the register, purchasing all the items.

"See anything else we should get her?" Paul asked.

Nell shook her head.

"What store should we go to next?" Paul asked.

"Paul, I could have gotten one or the other. It would have been fine."

"Yeah, but we could afford both. Let's get you something. Which store would you like to go to next? Pick one. Don't worry about the money."

"I don't need anything."

"Sure, you do. How about a new dress? Shoes? Anything you want!"

"I'm fine, really. There is no need for me to get anything…You do enough."

"I'm supposed to, I'm your husband. Tell me what you want, and I'll get it. Babe, it's perfectly fine. Don't worry about a budget. When it comes to you and Sharon, the sky is the limit. I've been saying that since we got back together. Each time we go to the mall, you rarely get anything for yourself. Starting today, things are going to be different. No ifs, ands, or buts, ya dig?"

Paul stared at Nell firmly as she glanced around uneasily.

"Nell," Paul spoke, his tone softer, "it's okay…I would have said something if it weren't…I just want to make you happy…"

He waited patiently. There were several people passing by talking and giggling, carrying their own bags.

"Okay, Paul," Nell stated. "Could we go to the bookstore?"

"Sure."

They entered the bookstore. Immediately, Nell's eyes lit up going into the section that contained the books on nursing. Paul placed the shopping bags on the floor and took Sharon into his arms. The little girl rested her head against her father's chest, closing her eyes to take a nap.

Nell began to grab a few books, using her fingers to turn the pages to quickly browse through each.

"Take your time," Paul stated, taking a quick glance at the other books along the aisle that led to an opening where the newspapers and magazines were kept. Paul continued his stroll, viewing the covers of the different sports and car magazines.

An older woman was standing nearby with a travel magazine in her hands. Two other women were discussing the costs of fruit from a grocery store advertisement.

"Aren't the nectarines cheaper at Jan's," the first lady asked the second.

"No, the ones at Hillsdale Grocers cost forty-nine cents a pound and you can get twelve lemons for fifty-nine cents," the other replied.

A man who looked to be in his thirties was seated at a small table doing a crossword puzzle.

"I want to be a daredevil when I grow up," a little boy bragged to his parents who were at the register to purchase their items. "Then, I can climb a tightrope too. I'll be the best there is!"

"Not until you become a doctor or lawyer first," his mother responded.

"Paul?"

"Right here, babe." Paul went back to the aisle where his wife was. He exchanged their daughter for the book, leaving them to purchase it at the register. After obtaining their new belongings, they placed them in the car. Soon, the family drove to Joel's place to watch the game.

"Thank you, Paul," Nell said.

"You're very welcome," Paul smiled, holding her hand with his free one, "and thank you for doing this. It means a lot." His breathing became deeper and steadier.

Joel's apartment complex was a few blocks from the mall. It was one of the better places with new amenities, an outdoor pool, and a lot of singles to go around. Most weekends, there were pool parties, and that weekend would be no exception. *Nell is going to be shocked, and I can't wait to see! If all goes well, maybe she would be up for us hosting a game or having more friends over. We have more than enough space to accommodate everyone, so I don't see why not!*

Paul quickly parked his vehicle into the parking lot of the Gardere Apartment complex. The apartments were all a single-story and painted a light blue. The landscape was pleasant with freshly cut grass and had an arrangement of flowers throughout the area. He could hear the splash coming from the back of the building, indicating that there were people enjoying the outdoor pool that sunny day.

Paul wished he had the opportunity to enjoy a nice swim, but he was there for something more important, the football game! Two of his favorite teams were playing against each other that day. It was the ultimate duo as far as he was concerned.

"Joel's apartment isn't too far, just follow me," Paul instructed, opening the door, and getting Sharon who was still sleepy into his arms. He led his wife on their walk until they reached apartment 134. Paul used his free hand to knock on the door.

Nell's eyes became watery as the door was opened to reveal a tall woman in her early twenties with brown hair and eyes dressed in a red and yellow polka dot bikini with a green towel wrapped around her waist.

"Margo," Paul exclaimed with a wide grin, "how's it hangin'?"

"Paul, so good to see you again," the woman beamed, her eyes almost bulging. "Is that Sharon?"

"Sure is," Paul spoke with confidence. "Told ya I'd bring my babydoll someday!" He stepped slightly to the side. "This is my lovely wife, Nell. Nell, this is Margo, Joel's old lady!"

"Nice to meet you, Nell," Margo said widening the door, "Come on in!"

The Boudreauxs followed Margo inside to a crowded living room, mostly composed of men who had eyes fixed on the television screen. There were at least two other women sitting amongst them. Most of the guests had plates of food in their laps consisting of hot dogs, pizza, potato chips, or chicken wings. Some had cans of beer and others had cans of soda.

"Hey, Paul," Joel called out from the couch. "Finally got the wife to come, I see! Cute kid, by the way!"

"Thanks," Paul responded. He faced his wife, "Nell, that's Joel, Greyson, Bobby, Larry, Eric, Tom, Laura, and Clair."

A few of the other guests took a glance, turning back to the television, some nodded, and two said, "hi."

"Would either of you like any refreshments?" Margo asked. "We have extra plates in the kitchen."

"No, thanks, we ate not too long ago," Paul responded.

Margo got two more chairs from the dining room for the Boudreauxs to sit, before taking her place next to Joel. They sat down together causing a rushed, rejuvenation to Paul. *Finally, I can say that Nell is with me and my friends. Please, God, make things continue to go well so we can do this again!*

Of all the women there, Clair was the most passionate about the football game, almost to the same extent as the men. From what Paul knew about each of the guys, only he, Joel, Greyson, and Bobby played the sport in high school. The others did different sports such as basketball, cross country, or baseball, but still enjoyed watching football. Laura was the only former cheerleader. Margo was a twirler and Clair was a member of the flag corps.

Nuzzling against the softness of his little girl's hair, Paul wondered if Sharon would ever be interested in any games once she got a little older. She certainly enjoyed throwing things.

Watching the teams on the screen run across the football field made Paul yearn for the good old days when he served as a quarterback at Wood Oak High School. Though a little older, he still managed to keep his athletic build and was still young and active. Sometimes, even when football season was over, Paul and his university friends would participate in a friendly game.

Savoring the moment, Paul took it all in, knowing what would lie ahead: returning to the armory for drill to fulfill his reserve duties. Paul hoped that Nell would be receptive to the idea of inviting new people into their own home to share long-lasting experiences. *I hope we can do it at least once...* In his racing mind, Paul began to think of the names of people to invite, the different foods to serve, and much more. The young man remembered the times his own parents had guests over for their events. Why shouldn't he in his own home? *Why not?* Everyone was being civil. Why couldn't that be the green light for him to do as he wished? It wasn't being unreasonable! Isn't that what most households did with their friends?

Nell remained quiet, her eyes fixed to the screen, leaving Paul to wonder what she was thinking. More than likely, she was possibly bored, not knowing what anything meant other than one team running from one end of the field to the other.

"You okay, honey?" Paul asked Nell.

"Yeah," Nell responded.

"So, you like going to South Aster College?" Margo asked Nell.

"Yeah," Nell answered.

"Most of us go to Camellia University with Paul," Margo told her. "Bobby goes to Azalea College. Eric and Tom go to Green Ash."

"Yeah, we all know each other because of this guy here," Greyson chuckled, pointing both index fingers towards Paul.

"Mr. Popular finally decided to settle down," Joel added. "Happy for you, man!"

"Paul is such a sweet guy," Laura added.

"Yeah, he's cool!"

A flush crept across Paul's cheeks. *They sure are laying it on thick...*

"How do you like Alabama, Nell?" Margo asked.

"It's okay," Nell answered.

"Actually, she loves it," Paul intervened. "She's being shy, is all."

Sharon shifted in his arms, opening her eyes.

"Ooh, she definitely has your eyes, Paul," Margo exclaimed as Sharon quickly clutched to her father tighter to turn away.

"Yep, but she gets her looks from her mother," Paul smiled as everyone resumed watching the game.

The phone began to ring, and Margo left her seat to respond.

"I can hold her," Nell whispered to Paul.

"It's fine," Paul said, giving Sharon a calming pat on the back. "Relax and enjoy yourself."

A few minutes later, Margo returned. In her hands was a cigarette and a lighter.

"I'm gonna head out for a smoke, anyone wanna come?" she asked the guests. Laura nodded, following her friend outside the apartment.

"Go, go, go," Clair shouted at the television screen watching one of the football players make a dash for a touchdown.

Unfortunately, the defense for the opposing team cut his run short, bringing him down at the one-yard line.

"Aww, man," Greyson shouted, almost choking on the hotdog he was in the middle of consuming.

"He was so close," Paul groaned.

Sharon began to shift in his arms again.

"Daddy, I have to tinkle," she said, climbing down from his lap.

"I'll take her," Paul told his wife, before walking the little girl to the restroom two rooms down the hall. He waited with his back turned away as Sharon went to relieve herself in the restroom.

"What are you doing?" Paul asked, entering the boys' restroom. The teens at Wood Oak High School had made it clear that Martin was only to use the last stall to the right of the boys' restroom. Regardless of Martin's compliance, the other students still made life difficult for him.

"Messing up the toilet so Martin won't be using our restroom again," one of the jocks said, carefully urinating on the toilet seat. Inside the toilet bowl was what was left of an entire roll of toilet paper soaking in water and urine. The floor was covered in discarded trash that had been collecting in the trashcan earlier that day.

"That'll only give him a reason to use one of ours," Paul groaned. "Mr. Sanford is gonna get mad again once he sees all this trash on the floor."

*"So what," Henry said. "Isn't that that n*****'s job to clean up behind everyone? If we're lucky, the principal'll give in and have Martin use the old outdoor toilet next to the gym."*

"Or not," Paul countered." It's been closed for a while and not even useable."

"Who cares! He's gross anyway. I bet he never washes his hair and everything he touches gets dirty."

"Daddy..."

Paul flushed the toilet and assisted Sharon in cleaning her hands. When they returned to the living room, Margo and Laura had returned and most eyes were still on the television screen. Sharon went into Nell's arms and sat in her mother's lap.

"Laura's cat had kittens not too long ago, would you like to see them?" Margo asked Sharon and Nell.

Sharon's eyes began to gleam. Bouncy with glee, she turned to face Nell who wasn't as quick to respond.

"Can I, Mommy?" Sharon pleaded.

"It's *may I*," Nell corrected her daughter. She faced Margo with a forced smile. "Maybe next time."

Immediately, Sharon's eyes began to water. Her chest began to quiver between sobs. Her bottom lip began to tremble.

"But I wanna see the kittens," the little girl sobbed, her voice getting louder. She began to bend and turn to get out of her mother's arms, shrieking.

Paul took Sharon into his arms.

Clair began to rub her brow. Bobby took in a deep breath and held it in. Tom's gaze flicked upward. Eric sighed heavily. *Damn!* It was game over for the Boudreauxs.

"Someone needs a nap," Paul said, his voice strained. "Sorry, but another time guys."

The way back to the car was no better. Sharon continued to cry loudly, flailing her arms and legs. Paul kept his gaze straight ahead, pretending not to see the onlookers who were staring and talking amongst themselves at their new form of entertainment. *God, I'm so embarrassed...* His pace began to accelerate with Nell following close behind. Paul's ears began to turn red. He winched, wishing to cover his face.

"I wanna see the kittens," Sharon screamed repeatedly.

Paul's face and neck began to feel impossibly hot.

"Get ready to take her," Paul instructed his wife as they approached the car. He handed Sharon over to Nell while he dug into his pants pocket to retrieve the car keys.

"Stop," Nell told the child who ignored her.

Almost dropping the car keys, Paul shoved the key into the right back passenger side, opening the door. While Nell was handling Sharon, Paul unlocked both front doors, and climbed inside. Once Nell was in, they began the drive home.

We are getting a babysitter when going to the next game, Paul thought, his chin dropping down slightly. He wanted to finish watching the game in peace, but that wasn't going to happen.

"Mommy, I wan...I wanna...see the kittens," Sharon wept.

Nell rested an arm against the car door, resting her head in the palm of her hand. Her posture sagged and her eyes were closed. With her other hand, she curled her fingers into a claw-like form that began to shake.

Maybe having another kid later wouldn't be a bad idea... I'm glad Nell talked some sense into me...I better think of something to calm Sharon down. Otherwise, Nell may not want anymore nor agree to go to another football get together. Paul rested his free hand on Nell's thigh, giving it a gentle squeeze. *I'll prove to her that I can still be a good father and husband...Here goes nothing!*

"Uh oh," Paul spoke, "We can't see the kittens if somebody is still crying."

Sharon choked back a sob. She wiped her face with the back of her hand.

"We don't want the kittens to be sad too," Paul continued. "They're gonna cry if they see you crying."

"We're seeing them?" Sharon asked with a sniffle. She was becoming curious and calmer.

It's working! Thank God!

"Sure, why not," Paul answered. "But you gotta show them that you're a big girl! They are watching right now."

"Where? I don't see them!"

"All around, like Santa Claus does. They can see us, but we can't see them, at least not now."

Sure, it wasn't true, but it sure was helping, and made Nell even slightly chuckle. Paul stopped the vehicle at the red light. Facing Nell, he mouthed, *pet store.*

"Not only are we gonna see the kittens, but puppies, fish, and other animals," Paul added. "They're all waiting to meet us. If you can wait a little longer, you, Mommy, and I will see them tomorrow after Daddy comes home from seeing Uncle Simon."

"Yay," Sharon squealed.

Paul continued the drive until they reached their home.

"You, okay?" Paul asked Nell.

"Yeah," Nell said, "it's hard sometimes…"

"I get it, especially now… We are definitely waiting!"

Nell widened her eyes, nodding repeatedly. Paul opened the door to the home, and they all entered. If he hurried to the living room, he could resume watching the rest of the football game, but he still had a lingering question.

"Babe," he asked, "is it okay if we could host a game here at home the weekend after I return home from the armory? I'd like to invite a few of my friends over and you could bring yours over too. We can hire a babysitter to watch Sharon until the game was over."

"I don't know, Paul...but, in all fairness, you never had a problem with me inviting the study group over...So, sure we can."

Chapter 14

"*Partners*?" Simon scoffed. "With a *woman*? What are they teaching you at that university? How would partnering with a nobody be beneficial in the long run? Are you intentionally wanting to fail?"

Paul sat outside with his uncle, Simon Dupont, on the back porch of his mansion on the outskirts of Camellia. He was surprised that the man was no longer cooped in his dark study within. Today, they were outside with a small table between them containing a glass pitcher of lemonade, glasses filled for both, and a tray of assorted fruit and desserts.

"I disagree," Paul countered. "Shelly Reynolds has a good record of being a passionate manager who cares about motivating her subordinates, having brilliant marketing strategies, and increasing profits for Pierre's since working there. Sure, she may have no national name yet, but she is doing very well in Wood Oak, Louisiana."

"That throwaway place is nothing more than a prime example of lowered standards," Simon persisted. "I should have followed my better judgement to have taken you out sooner instead of listening to that old fool, Abraham. All it amounted to was having my nephew become a juvenile delinquent who almost became a high school dropout. I will not even begin to express my distaste towards your use of drugs, alcohol, and loose women. But you didn't stop there. You had to impregnate and marry a colored woman. When, I ask you, will it all end? The Dupont fortune and legacy might as well burn to rubble!"

"Grandfather Beau thought little of my family in Wood Oak, but my father and his were successful."

"Is that what Andrew and Abraham said? That they were successful? With that tiny store and little bit of property?" Simon scoffed. "Neither would have had a leg to stand on had it not been for my brother and I and only because we loved our sister. That Shelly person would be no better to you than Andrew was to Helen, using you to reach a goal, unable to achieve it independently."

"Well, I still have plans underway to revive Sal's and Shelly's the best option I have for Wood Oak, so we'd be using each other."

"Speak no further, you make a poor case for yourself and this Shelly person."

"It's my decision and money," Paul groaned, his frustrations mounting. He tilted his head, closing his eyes briefly. He regretted telling his uncle anything of his plans. Still, with an increased internal temperature and heartbeat, Paul remained calm and focused. What was the benefit of Sal's remaining vacant and untouched when he was still paying property taxes? It could have been sold off years ago, as his uncle recommended. Yet, the property had been in the Boudreaux family since the parish first came into existence, making it one of the oldest buildings there.

Weary, Paul took a sip from the glass of lemonade set before him.

"My little girl sometimes reminds me of mother," Paul said to lighten the conversation, if even for himself. "She also has a strong passion for animals. Remember Lucy? She was a beautiful tuxedo cat."

Simon cocked his head to the side at the recollection.

"Lucy was our cat but was more of the neighborhood cat," Paul recalled. "She hated staying indoors too long, but always came back faithfully to eat her dinner and sleep in my bed. Yeah, she would annoy me when she slept on my legs, but I sure do miss her. I thought about getting Sharon a cat, but I must see what Nell thinks first."

"Are you not the man of the house? Do as you wish."

"Well, I do value my wife's opinion."

"She is a woman; she has none."

"I wish you'd stop talking like that, Uncle," Paul sighed. "You always cared about Mother, valuing what she wanted, and she was a woman."

"I will always remain loyal to my sister," Simon told him. "Others, I could care less."

Paul pulled himself up from his seat.

"I understand," he said. "I better head out. Nell, Sharon, and I will be heading to the pet shop to look at animals. We will be having a get together at our home soon to watch the football game. I know you're not into sports nor like associating much with outsiders, but you're invited to come, if up to it."

After departing his uncle's mansion, Paul returned home to pick up his family to take them to the pet store. Sharon was in a much brighter mood, swaying her legs enthusiastically throughout the drive, and moving from side to side singing along to the music on the radio.

"I hope we aren't leaving with a pet snake," Nell whispered to Paul, who began to park the car in the parking lot, "or worse yet, a tarantula."

"Imagine one slowly walking on the couch," Paul joked, using his free hand to mimic the movements of a spider on her leg.

"Stop it, Paul," Nell cried out swatting his hand away.

Paul laughed, leaving the vehicle. He waited for Nell to help Sharon from the backseat, and they all entered the pet store. The pet store had not only animals, but pet supplies. The flower shop next door was separated by a single door that was open and inviting. Sharon skipped her way to where the cats were. Paul made a beeline towards the birds. He began whistling, making note of their different breeds: parakeets, orange winged amazons, lovebirds, *cockatoos*…His mind getting vulgar, Paul snickered.

"May I help you, sir?" a staff member asked Paul.

"Just looking around, thanks," Paul answered, passing through the door into the flower shop. He saw numerous flowers and a beautifully crafted water fountain that was filled with water.

"Look, Mommy, a flower garden," Sharon called out from the doorway. Almost dragging her mother behind her, she led Nell towards Paul. She let go of her mother's hand, leaving both parents to explore more of the facility and its beautiful flowers.

"Nice finding you here, Foxy Mama," Paul began to flirt, wrapping an arm around his wife. "Someone must enjoy keeping a gentleman waiting. Welcome to the place only second to the beautiful Garden of Eden."

Nell cracked a smile, "I don't think the wait has been as long as someone is making it!"

"C'mon, babe, let's have a little fun," Paul whispered, sneaking to give her bottom a squeeze. "How about we somewhere private to fulfill our sexual fantasies to the fullest…"

Covering her mouth with her hand, Nell roared with laughter.

"In your dreams," she whispered with a bit of laughter. "We're not doing that here!"

"C'mon," Paul whispered, his smile impish, "there's gotta be a private room somewhere. It's been a while since we've done it somewhere new. Stop pretending to be so innocent. I see that smile!"

"Get lost! We're not here for that!"

Nell gave Paul a playful shove and proceeded to briskly walk away. Paul pretended to chase after her, resulting in them both laughing out loud. Finally, Nell turned around, raising a hand to the side of her mouth.

Wait until we get home, she mouthed.

Paul tossed his head back, momentarily closing his eyes. He clutched his chest as if he had been shot.

Nell laughed more, following Sharon back into the pet store.

Paul remained behind. The flowers sure were pretty, like Nell. He was glad that they lived in an area that had plenty of azaleas throughout the city, making it a place that was photogenic. The camellias were also as impressive during certain seasons.

I'm gonna start keeping my camera in the car, Paul thought. *I want to capture every moment and relive them as much as I possibly can.*

Minutes later, Paul reentered the pet shop to find Nell and Sharon gazing at the kittens near the window.

"Enjoying the kittens, babydoll?" Paul asked.

"Can we take one home?" Sharon begged, her eyes pleading.

Paul gazed at Nell who shrugged her shoulders. Although Sharon loved her stuffed animals, she still needed to comprehend what it was like to have a real one. She needed to understand what foods and drinks a cat would need for its diet and how cats behaved. They could practice and see how things would go from there. That sounded reasonable, but would it be to Sharon?

"Let's make a deal," Paul suggested. "How about you and I take a few days to learn about cats, like what they like to eat, what they like to play, and such. Then, when the time is right, we can take one home. In the meantime, you must be a good little girl and listen to Mommy and Daddy. Deal?"

Sharon nodded.

Good, Paul thought. *That's a nice lesson to teach her how to have patience and not rush into things. She'll learn about cats in no time…Hmm, Lucy was pretty old when I was around Sharon's age, but she lived until I was about nine… Wasn't Uncle Simon the one who gave her to Mother?*

Alone, Paul waited on top of the teacher's desk. Nell was running late, or perhaps, she didn't want to be there. Paul swore underneath his breath, recollecting the night before. They had gone all the way, and it was nerve wracking, wondering what Nell thought.

Paul thought of Patricia Weber. She had been his first. She was a high school junior cheerleader and Paul was a freshman. Pat was pretty with black hair and green eyes. She and her boyfriend had split up, so she began dating Paul. Things were great, until Paul discovered that she rekindled her relationship with her ex, leaving their relationship. However, the joke was on them, her parents decided to move away, taking her with them. Unfortunately, while it was sweet revenge, it did, in a deep place, break Paul's heart, finalizing the end to that chapter in his life.

The doorknob began to turn with the door opening. Nell slipped in. Paul beamed, pushing himself off the table. He greeted her with a kiss that was returned.

"How do you feel?" Paul asked.

"I'm not sure," Nell answered. "Strange, I guess…"

"It feels weird at first, but once you get used to it, it feels good," Paul told her as they both sat down on the teacher's desk.

"Funny thing is…" Nell spoke, "I didn't expect to see you here today…I didn't want to be dumped or see that I had been had…I was scared, really…after hearing so many stories about girls having sex for the first time and the guy taking off…I didn't want that person to be you, not after the risks, the I love you's, and of all things, last night."

"I get it. To be honest, I was scared too, to take a risk. People are always using each other for gain, like popularity, money, revenge, or whatnot. I saw early on that none of that was true in this relationship…and, I've been through it all. Since it was your first time, I thought it would be nice to make it as special as possible. I hope it was as nice and enjoyable for you as it was for me."

Paul smiled seeing Nell do the same. The school bell began to chime.

"I'll see you in class," Nell said kissing him. "I love you."

"I love you too," Paul said returning the kiss. "See you there and on our date later tonight."

Chapter 15

"Ralph is lucky we got a B on that project," Greyson said, cracking his knuckles on the outside of the business building later that Monday afternoon. "I wanted to pound his face into oblivion when he began stuttering during his parts of the presentation. The guy speaks perfectly until it's time to present! Geeze! What a skuzz!"

"That was good thinking, Paul," Joel added, "using Ralph's blunder as a ploy to say that he couldn't believe what a wonderful product the shoelaces were at affordable prices! Now, we all can rest easy. I'm glad it's over! I hate group projects!"

"Me too," Paul agreed, letting out a huge breath. "Ralph must have been more nervous than anyone because he had more to lose. That's probably why he was teamed up with us, to help him."

"That aint right," Greyson grumbled, his tone sharp. "Why sacrifice our grades to save that chump? If he's not smart enough to do things on his own, he doesn't deserve to have the same degree the rest of us are working so hard to get!"

"Might as well chill out," Paul told him. "Like Joel said, it's over. Now, is the time to focus on our other classes and cleaning all those rifles and machine guns soon at the armory."

"Don't forget to add in a few tables of pool in between," Greyson added. "I want another chance to earn some of that money that I lost back!"

"Go ahead and hand me the money now," Joel laughed. "I won't have to worry about next month's rent and could probably talk the apartment manager into adding some shag carpeting."

Cindy approached the trio, causing the conversation to become quieter.

"Paul, may I speak to you in private?" she asked.

"Sure," Paul said, walking with her a few yards away.

"Sorry I didn't make it for the show," Cindy told him. "But, thank you… for being there when I wasn't strong enough to go myself… I never expected for you to show after you told me you probably weren't going either."

"I'm sorry myself. Last week, I had a bit of bad news … But things have a way of clearing themselves up and even Nell went. So, I assume things are getting better?"

"Yes, I had time to reflect on a lot of things…I was so tired of putting so much into relationships and being tossed away, like someone who had no feelings whatsoever. I was at home that night, thinking about ways to end my life. At first, I thought about driving my car off a bridge or swallowing a bunch of pills. If nobody cared about me, why should I? But you called saying that you were at the show for me…but, I didn't believe you. I wanted to, that night… So, today, I asked the people who also had work at the show, and they said, you had shown up. Nell is such a lucky person. I guess, I envy her a lot because she has someone like you all to herself. Even though things ended with us, I'm still happy to call you a friend."

"Thanks, Cindy," Paul said giving her a hug.

"Thanks for being honest with me," Cindy said, her eyes tearing, "and being nice about Jacob too."

Paul watched as she reentered the art building. It was almost that time. He said his goodbyes to his other friends and began to walk to the parking lot. The sun was shining brightly and there was a pleasant breeze. Reaching into his pants pocket, Paul pulled out a stick of gum, unwrapping it, and sticking it into his mouth. The minty flavor slightly stung his taste buds in a good way, causing him to nod, reflecting on the freshness. Paul spotted Wilma where he had left her earlier that day. His smile slowly faded, viewing the long crooked horizontal line that had been deeply keyed along his beloved car. Nearly fainting and choking on his own gum, Paul's eyes shot wider as he began to yell out a long rage-fueled number of cuss words.

"Who keyed my fuckin' car?" Paul demanded while a few bystanders began to gawk his way.

Color draining from his face, Paul touched the line that ruined Wilma's perfect blue paint with his shaky hand. He needed to repair the damage soon, but he also had the task of picking up his daughter. Paul hurried to examine the rest of his vehicle, not finding any additional damage. He hurled himself inside, slamming his fists against the steering wheel. Of course, there was the usual long lines of cars filled with people waiting to leave campus, fueling his anger and suspicions further. Any one of them could be the culprit. Paul inched his car further along the crowded road.

Why Wilma, Paul thought almost weeping. *Who could have done such a thing to a beautiful car? I'm gonna murder whoever did this! I bet it was probably Cindy's ex, Ralph, or some other chump!*

Beep! Beep!

The sound of the car horns were getting on his last nerve, causing his body to tense.

"Shut up," Paul roared from inside the vehicle, soon spotting a brown four-door vehicle one car ahead of him to the left. Paul drove his vehicle forward, examining the vehicle next to his. Inside, there was a black man with a mustache, medium sized afro, and sideburns. He had black glasses, a plaid red, black, and white shirt with a pocket containing pencils and pens.

A heaviness expanding to his core, Paul's widening eyes locked with the man's whose mouth made an ugly twist.

Fuck you, the man mouthed from his vehicle.

Instantly, Paul's face turned into a sneer upon the recognition of the man. His fingers curling and blood pressure rising, Paul growled his enemy's name, "Martin!"

Gripping his steering wheel, Paul began to wait for the person ahead of him to move forward more so he could veer his own vehicle into his rival's.

Martin lifted his hand to lower all his fingers except the middle finger.

It was on! Paul no longer cared about the person ahead of him nor any other driver. With adrenaline coursing through his veins, he sharply turned his steering wheel, hoping to plow into Martin's vehicle, but the other vehicle merged into another lane, missing the impact.

Beep! Beeeppp! The driver behind Martin's vehicle blasted their horn, barely missing Paul's car by centimeters.

"Move out of my way," Paul yelled, attempting to merge into the lane with the other driver yelling his own expletives.

Martin's car merged again, quickly heading towards an exit street, resulting in Paul roaring with anger that he missed the opportunity to reach his enemy. Now, he had the additional difficulty of exiting the lane that led to the exit to his daughter's daycare. Paul struggled to get back into his original lane, ending there two missed exits later and having to take a different route to his destination. Throughout the drive, he had numerous questions such as, *"What is Martin doing in Camellia, of all places? When did he get here? How? I bet the chump keyed my car, the jerk! Wait till I get my hands on him!"*

After picking up his daughter, Paul waited impatiently for Nell to return home. As much as he wanted to grab a chair or two to flip them over, he didn't want to scare Sharon who was lounging in the living room watching a children's program. Unable to sit still, Paul began to pace back and forth throughout the home. His frustrations mounting, his thoughts began to blank. Then, it hit him, causing a freak out. *Was Nell aware that Martin was in town?* Were there secrets? *Intimate secrets?*

"God, no," Paul bellowed, accidentally hitting his toe against the dining room table leg. Pain surging, Paul clutched his leg, screaming.

"Daddy?" Sharon's concerned voice called out.

"D-d-daddy's fine, babydoll," Paul called out, followed by a muffled groan. "I hit my toe…"

The young man sunk into a nearby chair. His foot continued to suffer a surge of discomfort. Pursing his lips, Paul closed his eyes, leaning forward in a grimace.

"I'm home," Nell's voice called out, followed by the sound of the door closing and keys being placed upon the kitchen counter.

Nearly limping, Paul made his way there, watching his wife casually put on an apron, as if she were innocent. Of course, Nell looked beautiful as usual, but Paul was in no mood to be enchanted by her beauty now. If he weren't so disgusted, he would have done his usual flirting.

"Hey, handsome," Nell smiled, giving him a quick smooch. "Why are you limping? Sit down; I'll get you whatever you need."

Paul sunk into a nearby barstool.

"My car got keyed today," Paul informed her, studying every move his wife made. "I'm gonna have to take it to the shop to get fixed."

Nell's head jerked back; her mouth fell open. She hurried outside and soon reentered with her hand covering her mouth.

"I didn't notice anything when I came in because it's on the driver's side. Paul, what happened?"

"Someone keyed it on purpose, and I know who did," Paul told her. "It was *Martin…Martin Parker*. Remember him from Wood Oak? He's here. My question is, *why*? Did you know?" He focused on Nell's face to see if she possibly could be hiding anything, but she appeared to be as surprised as he was when he found out himself.

"No, I knew nothing about it. Are you sure it was Martin and not a look-alike? Why would he be here of all places? That would be a strange coincident."

"Of course, I'm sure! He's the nerd with the thick glasses, and pocket filled with writing utensils!"

"He's not the only person in the world to wear thick glasses and have pockets filled with writing utensils…"

"How does he know about *us* living here? What's he doing at my school? How does he know what car I drive? Nell, are you telling me the truth about what you know?"

"I am! I haven't spoken to him since high school! Maybe he found out from his brother or Claudine. Those two are engaged and like to talk."

"Since when was his brother engaged to your sister?"

"They've kept in touch and Tyrone moved up to Illinois to be near Claudine about a year ago. I assumed Martin stayed back in Wood Oak with their parents."

"How does your sister like to talk, but nobody in your family mentioned Martin being here?"

"I just started talking to them again. Everyone's busy helping Claudine plan her wedding and going to work."

Paul's nerves quickly began to calm down. *So, she hasn't been seeing him without my knowing...But, I still don't like that he knows about us, and he's gonna pay for what he did to my car!*

"Ask your sister where Martin lives so I can pay him a visit to key his face like he did my car," Paul uttered.

"You better not. You don't want to go to jail, do you?"

"It would be worth it. I'd turn his face into a roadmap!"

"Please don't... Think about it...Can you blame him? You did bully him in high school, badly."

"Yeah, but I apologized like I was asked to. That was years ago. He had plenty of time to get over it."

"Well, sometimes forgiveness takes time..."

Paul scoffed.

"What about me? How'd you expect for me to react? He wanted you as much as I did. I won; he needs to get over it."

"*You won?* What does that mean? This isn't one of those football games to win."

"Why defend him so much? Last time I checked, you were my wife, not his. It's not my fault he isn't me, though I am happy that I am not him!"

Nell rolled her eyes.

"Just, promise me," she said," that you won't do anything to him. I'll pay for the repairs—"

"Yeah, with *my* money, huh? No, he's gonna pay with his own! I'll have a copy of the bill waiting for him and that's if I don't punch his face in before he has a chance to see it."

Nell released a long exhale, resuming working on dinner. Paul entered the living room, slumping down on the couch to join Sharon in watching the television show. His eyelids getting heavy, a nap sure seemed that it would be a good idea to Paul. He began to fold his arms against his chest and close his eyes while he took slow and steady breaths. He slept until Nell woke him for the family to eat dinner in the dining room. Paul dug into his macaroni and cheese, savoring the cheesy goodness that made him consider a second helping, possibly a third. *Mmm, mmm, I'm gonna have to work out a lot if I keep eating like this.*

"While you were sleeping," Nell spoke, "I called my dad and asked about Martin. He said that Martin had gotten a scholarship to go to the same school as you, but he is in the medical program to become a pediatrician. Isn't that something? A doctor! Wow!"

A doctor! Paul's lips pinched flat as the words began to sink in. *And Nell a nurse!* It sounded like Martin had more in common with his wife than he did, almost as if they were destined to be together in some capacity, something Paul solely wanted for himself. *Over my dead body if Martin is weaseling his way into taking my wife away from me. Why did Nell seem so excited to hear about Martin's major? Without that scholarship, he'd be deeply in debt, like all the other medical students who don't come from money. How is that impressive? I'm the better choice in every way! I'm going to the same school, but in a different department! At least I have good looks and don't need glasses or a pocketful of pencils and pens. I bet he could never throw a football!"*

"All this time you've never run into him?" Nell asked Paul.

"No, the medical school isn't on the main campus," Paul responded. "It's downtown…"

"Well, I will apologize for him," Nell said. "I'm sure that once he forgives you, he'll feel bad about what he did, if he was the person who keyed your car."

You would think that, huh, Paul thought, taking a sip of sweet tea from his glass. He picked up a piece of his baked chicken and began eating it.

"How about your school?" Paul asked, "He might be showing up there too."

"I wouldn't know. I haven't seen him in years."

"He has a mustache and grew his hair and sideburns out."

"Oh, that's different for sure…"

"Stay away from him, okay… I don't want him to hurt neither you nor Sharon because he holds a grudge against me. Sure, he may be going to a medical school, but what sane doctor would key someone's car? I want you two to be safe."

Nell opened her mouth as if starting to disagree, stopping short as Paul began to raise an eyebrow.

"Okay…"

Chapter 16

Leaning back in his chair, Paul began to yawn.

Taking in a deep breath and holding it briefly, Mrs. Miller turned Paul's way with a pinched face before returning her gaze to the front of the classroom where Martin stood.

"Continue Martin," Mrs. Miller sighed.

His hands clenched, Martin continued his report on a book that he had been assigned. He spoke only three words when another audible yawn interrupted him. Most eyes faced Paul, but he only smirked as a few classmates began to snicker.

"This is boring," Henry groaned, letting out his own yawn. "Can't we move on to the next person?"

"Mr. Wilkerson," Mrs. Miller sneered, "mind your manners when one of your classmates is speaking! One more outburst and it's detention!"

"Yes, ma'am," Henry grumbled.

Once more, Martin attempted his speech only to be interrupted again with another yawn from the left of the classroom. Yet again, everyone faced Paul.

"It wasn't me," Paul told the class that began to laugh.

Eyes turned back to the front, then there was another yawn from the right. The game had already begun. The day before, the football players had all agreed to yawn during Martin's report. Whoever yawned the most before Mrs. Miller said or did anything would win. So far, Henry was ahead four yawns, but was now out of the game.

"If I hear one more yawn, it's an automatic detention," Mrs. Miller warned the class, only to get a defiant yawn in return, followed by more snickers.

"That's a detention, Mr. Allen!"

"It wasn't me," one of the jocks protested.

"You too, Ms. Perkins!"

"I didn't do anything, Mrs. Miller," Nancy objected. "I didn't even yawn!"

"You laughed and anyone else who laughs will also get a detention!"

"That's not fair!"

"Do you want a second?" Mrs. Miller demanded.

Nancy began to sulk in her chair with her arms folded.

After class, Paul waited at the classroom entrance with his head resting against the wall. Nancy was sobbing and complaining to her friends about the unfairness of her detention. Her chest quivering, she stacked her books on top of Paul's, continuing her sobs.

Mrs. Miller is always ruining our fun, Paul thought. He didn't get caught, but he didn't win either. Henry exited the classroom grumbling, but at least he won, meaning each of the jocks had to give him either a smoke or one of their lemon bars from the cafeteria.

Paul began his walk down the crowded hallway, moving between the students. A scrunched paper flew across the hallway.

Unexpectedly, another student was shoved forward, almost losing his grip on the books and papers he was carrying.

"Move," a voice was heard not so far behind him.

There were some jeers, chuckles, and chattering. Paul turned around to see Martin walking to his next class, *until he was not. He had fallen on the floor, attempting to collect himself. Someone shoved him in the rear with their foot, causing him to fall further.*

"Idiot!"

*"Learn to walk, n*****!"*

The cafeteria fared no better with students taking food from Martin's tray, flinging it off the floor, or using the food to dump on his clothes.

"How much longer you think he's gonna sit there?" Henry inquired at the table occupied by the jocks, cheerleaders, and other popular teens.

"You think if I take this ketchup and smear it on his face, that it'll make him look like a clown?" one of the jocks asked.

"Nah, he's too dark to see anything."

"He reminds me of burnt toast."

Paul resumed eating his food as the conversations continued.

"Look, his girlfriend is here!"

Paul spotted Nell walking in the cafeteria, missing a wadded paper flying her way. She sat down next to Martin.

"She's so stupid," Nancy said. "Why would either of them want to be here?"

Paul watched as Nell took a napkin to wipe the food off Martin's face.

"Oooh, isn't that sweet," one of the jocks mocked. "Too bad I got to get rid of the leftover food on my tray."

He approached the two, dumping his tray on top of Nell's and using it to shove Martin's inches away from the pair. Henry and another jock went next, slamming their fists against the table, causing it to shake violently. Observers began to gasp, point, talk, and laugh as more people from Paul's table joined. Among the last, Paul took his tray. He had to do something next; all eyes were on him. He had some leftover garlic bread and spaghetti sauce. He tilted his tray, resulting in the bread and sauce spilling on the table that Martin and Nell occupied.

Later that day, Paul saw Martin and Nell again at the back of the school. There were two other black students with them who he knew were their younger siblings: Claudine and Tyrone.

"Fight them," Tyrone told his older brother. "They aren't ever going to stop if you allow them to keep doing this to you."

"Shut up," Martin grumbled. "Fighting back won't help. You fight back and still get picked on."

"I hate this school," Claudine said. "I'd rather drop out than continue being here!"

"Stop saying that, Claudine," Nell told her. "That's what they want us to do!"

"Well, it's working!" Claudine said.

"Let's go home," Martin instructed his brother who began to ball his fists.

*"The next c****** that messes with me is gonna get the white smacked out of him," Tyrone grumbled.*

"Shut up," Martin told him. "Let's go home before you get in trouble for getting into another fight."

"Looks like they are having another meeting," Henry said, jogging towards Paul. "I bet they are planning on burning down our school, like they did theirs."

"Boudreaux, Wilkerson, on the field now," Coach Anderson ordered from the other side of the fence that divided the football field from the school's building.

On Tuesday, Paul took his car in to repair the scratches and Nell later dropped him off on his campus. He assured her that he and Sharon would be able to catch a ride back home with Greyson. While most of the day went without incident, neither Joel nor Greyson took the news lightly when they heard about Paul's vehicle being keyed.

"Once you find out where this bozo lives, let me know," Greyson stated, balling one of his hands into a fist and hitting it against the palm of the other. "I know a guy who drives a dump truck, and he'll dump all sorts of trash on his property!"

"Sure… but give me a minute to rip that mustache off his face so I can scratch his car with it," Paul added, cracking his knuckles.

"We should go to the medical school and teach him a thing or two," Joel said.

"That defeats the purpose," Paul grumbled. "The medical staff would only pamper him back to normal and we could get in trouble."

"He didn't get in trouble for what he did," Greyson told Paul. "He keyed your car in broad daylight, and everyone acted like they didn't see a thing! He's only gonna do it again or do something worse the next time he sees your car. He knows where you park your car, and you know which part of campus he's on and where to find his! This needs to be taken care of right now or he'll think you're a chump. He's already proven that he is one by doing it while you were gone, but you can show him that your bigger than he is whether you're there or not. We could have him buckling in his boots. Act now or regret it later!"

Greyson struck Paul as having many valid points, but he also made a promise to Professor Kingsley to stay out of trouble. He had been doing good for a while, and yet, Martin had to sabotage things. What if the man wanted a brawl to demand respect? Paul certainly wasn't going to be made a fool out of, not even years later, by some square who considered himself Joe Cool because he had some sideburns and a mustache!

"Let's go," Paul said, his muscles tightening in readiness.

Holding his chin high, Greyson pumped his fist in the air, "Right on!"

"I'll have to meet you guys there," Joel said. "Professor Kingsley asked me to go to his office and I said I would be there. I wouldn't be surprised if he were late, but I know a shortcut to the medical school, so I won't be too long!"

"That's fine," Paul replied. "We can drive around the lot to find Martin's car before we leave him a little gift."

"Stop wasting time," Greyson groaned. "Have you two forgotten about the traffic? We have to go now, or we'll miss him before he leaves for the day!"

Leaving Joel behind, Greyson drove Paul towards the medical school located downtown. Traffic was growing at a steady pace, but at least it was moving. Once they reached their exit, they drove to the parking lot of the medical school to begin scanning for Martin's vehicle.

The lot was bigger and more crowded than Paul had imagined. There were several people walking around in white lab coats, white nursing uniforms, or regular street clothes.

"Any of these cars look familiar?" Greyson asked, steadily driving down the lot.

"Not yet," Paul said looking at all the different colors, searching for the brown vehicle. They continued to drive until they had to stop the car to allow several people to cross into another section of the lot. Paul breathed steadily until he saw another group of people walking to their vehicles.

"That's the guy," Paul cried out, spotting Martin as the only black male walking next to a black woman in the group.

Greyson slowed down until he came to a complete stop, parking the car.

Martin and the woman broke away from the rest of the group, walking to an unfamiliar white vehicle. The woman appeared to be flirting with Martin, giggling and smiling, causing Paul to feel sick to his stomach. He wasn't sure if it was because the sight of the man made him sick or that someone could potentially be interested in such a geeky looking man or maybe both. If the two were shagging, at least, the man wasn't occupying his time with his eyes still set on Nell. Regardless, Paul and Greyson didn't make the drive for nothing, and Martin needed to pay for what he did to Paul's car! Martin had disgraced him in front of everyone by having the audacity to key his vehicle and now it was Paul's turn to embarrass Martin. Not only was he going to key the fool's car but humiliate the man in front of the woman who was interested in him. If she saw how weak he was, it would crush him!

Greyson and Paul rushed out of Greyson's vehicle while Martin opened the driver's door to the woman's car, allowing her inside. Greyson grabbed Martin from behind dragging him to the opening of the lot. Paul delivered a punch to Martin's stomach, causing him to have the wind knocked out of him.

"This is for my car you jerk," Paul shouted, delivering another hit.

Instantly, the black woman exited her vehicle, rushing towards the trio.

"Martin," she cried out. She took her purse and swung it at both Paul and Greyson. "Leave him alone! Get your hands off him!"

Greyson held firmly while Martin struggled to escape. Bystanders began to point and head in their direction. Paul swore under his breath, receiving another smack to his side by the woman's purse. He grabbed the purse strap, snatching the purse away from the woman and hurling it to the ground. Martin leaned his head forward, then sharply backwards, hitting Greyson in the face with a headbutt. Greyson released a sharp pain-ridden yelp as he grabbed his nose, freeing Martin from his clutches.

"That's what you get, you fat son-of-a-bitch," Martin told Greyson before raising his fists. He hurried towards Paul and the two began to circle one another.

"Help," the woman continued to cry out. "Somebody get security!"

"What's going on?" a woman wondered out loud.

"Hey, there's a fight!"

"Where's security?"

"Come on," Paul egged Martin on, taking a missed swing. "Let's finish this."

"Well, I'll be damned! So, it *is* Paul Boudreaux in the flesh," Martin chuckled, taking a swing that Paul dodged. "Still beating up on as many black folk as humanly possible, huh? Even after raping and ruining the life of the girl I liked!"

"What?" Paul countered, his mouth falling open. *"Raped who? I never raped anyone!"*

"Call it whatever you want, I know what it was! *Everyone* knew I liked Nell, including you, and you took full advantage of your whiteness to do what you did to her! Even after all that, you slept with half of the women on the university's campus, you womanizer!"

"I'd never do any of that, you psychopath!"

"Nell deserved a much better fate than what was given to her! She was the sweetest person I've ever known, and you ruined her life," Martin rushed forward, landing a punch on Paul's jaw, causing him to stumble back.

Paul cried out, grabbing his jaw as Martin proceeded to deliver more punches. Paul backhanded Martin, resulting in his glasses falling to the ground. Martin grabbed Paul's shirt and Paul grabbed his arms, leading to both men falling to the ground after losing their footing.

"I'm not letting you get away with anything else," Martin shouted. "I'm gonna tell Nell everything you've done behind her back! God, I should have kicked your ass years ago!"

Both men continued to deliver a series of blows towards the other until two brave men began to pull them apart.

"Get out of my way," Greyson yelled at two other men who tried to keep him at bay.

"You'll pay," Martin shouted at Paul. "Out of all the girls, why Nell? Why, you evil, white monster!" He grabbed Paul's neck, causing him to choke. "I'll kill you!"

Paul grabbed Martin's hands. Martin's grip was strong and restricted his air supply. Lightheaded, Paul's vision became blurry and the sounds around him grew faint.

"Alright buddy, enough," a voice said.

The next thing Paul could remember was coughing and gasping for air. He rolled to his side, holding his throat.

"Paul, we gotta get out of here," Greyson shouted, picking Paul up by the back of his shirt and almost dragging him back towards the vehicle.

Three men tried to block Greyson's path, but the young man pushed forward, using his size a strength to his advantage.

"Move," Greyson shouted, nearly tackling the three men and other spectators who were blocking the path. Paul regained the balance of his feet.

"You two, stop," one man in a security uniform ordered. He and another security officer rushed out of the medical facility into the parking area.

Ignoring them, Greyson and Paul kept running. One man attempted to block Greyson, but quickly fell over from the impact. The two security officers inched closer. Patting his pants pocket, Greyson began swearing out loud. He ran past his own vehicle with Paul following him.

"Shit," Greyson roared. "I can't find my keys!"

"Hey, watch where you're going," Paul warned his friend.

But it was too late, Paul watched helplessly as Greyson went tumbling down, falling over a broken piece of concrete. Falling to his feet, Greyson yelled in agony as he grabbed ahold of his leg, bringing it to his midsection.

"Come on," Paul shouted, lowering himself to grab ahold of his friend, but he was too heavy to carry.

Greyson released his leg, pulling himself back to his feet seconds before one of the security officers grabbed him. Without someone to grab, the officer fell forward and landed on the concrete. Paul and Greyson rushed to the road when Paul spotted Joel's grey four-door car driving close to the parking lot. Catching his second wind, Paul rushed to the vehicle that stopped abruptly. He opened the front passenger door, climbing inside. A little more out of shape, Greyson trailed behind, limping, sweating, and gasping for air.

"What's going on?" Joel asked, his eyes darting between his friends and the security officers.

"We need to get out of here," Paul told him. "I'll explain later!"

Panicking, Joel pressed his foot against the accelerator, distancing the car further away from Greyson.

"What are you doing, stop the car," Paul shouted.

Joel slammed his foot on the breaks, causing the car to squeal to a sudden stop. The car behind his almost collided into Joel's back bumper. Irate, the driver blew his car horn while Joel waited impatiently for Greyson to catch up. He barely made it inside Joel's vehicle when the car went flying down the street, almost plunging into a bus that had stopped to drop off passengers.

Cussing out loud, Joel sped down the street. Paul rested his head against the headrest, gasping for air and trying to control his racing heart. He turned around to the back passenger seats to see Greyson leaning forward, struggling to breathe himself.

Darn it, Paul thought, lifting, and slamming his head back onto the headrest.

"What did you two numbskulls do?" Joel demanded.

"What do you think?" Paul responded, dryly. "We were in the middle of kicking that jerk's ass until some idiot called security."

"They probably got my darn license plate number to start pointing the fingers at me too," Joel grumbled. "What happened to using Greyson's car?"

"He dropped his keys," Paul answered.

"Great, now they can identify him and take his car, idiots," Joel told him.

"I wouldn't have dropped them if it weren't for that stupid woman hitting me with her purse," Greyson responded.

"So, you allowed *a woman* to overpower you with *her purse*?" Joel uttered. "Maybe she should have played defense on your high school's football team instead of you! We are in deep trouble, if this ever gets back to the wrong person and I'm sure it will. Damn, you guys can't do anything right!"

"Could you take me to the daycare center," Paul asked. "I need to get Sharon. Whatever you do, no word about this to Nell or anyone else!"

Joel continued to grumble about how stupid Paul and Greyson were but granted Paul's request to pick up his daughter. There was no way that Paul was going to mention his misdeed to his wife and prayed that she would never find out.

Chapter 17

"Explain yourselves, *now!*"

"He keyed my car," Paul answered, "because we've hated each other since high school. I married the girl he wanted and he's still bitter about it."

"Do you have evidence that Mr. Parker keyed your vehicle?" Dean Kelly asked, folding his arms over his chest, staring the young man directly in the eye.

Paul, Greyson, and Joel had been asked to go to the Dean's office. They were in serious trouble after being identified by witnesses and evidence left behind on the scene. The dean was known to be a no-nonsense man, almost reminding Paul of his Uncle Simon in his firm demeanor. In fact, both men knew each other and had conducted business in the past. The man was bald with blue eyes and wore a business suit that was as tailor made as they come. His office was well-maintained, possibly without the smallest trace of dust. He had numerous plaques of his accomplishments hanging on the wall, a shelf filled with books, a large desk, and executive chairs.

"No, sir," Paul responded, an empty feeling at the pit of his stomach. "But it *was* Martin. No one else would have a reason to damage my car other than him, given our negative history. On the same day that my car got keyed, we ran into each other not too far off campus. He looked like he was trying to leave the scene, saw me, and made an obscene gesture. That was enough proof in my book."

"*But not for me,*" Dean Kelly replied. "A gesture means nothing. Therefore, you *assumed* it was Mr. Parker and invited your friends to aid in the attack of a probable innocent man... I have a good mind to expel all three of you! Without thinking, you three single-handedly compromised the good name of the university and have opened doors for Mr. Parker to open a lawsuit against yourselves *and* the university, in what he is claiming to be a racially motivated attack!"

"*Racially motivated attack?*" Paul gasped. "This had absolutely nothing to do with race! My wife and daughter—"

"Enough," the dean interrupted, his voice stern. "All three of you can thank your prominent families for being your saving graces this only time around. However, one more incident and all three of you are finished at this university, especially you, Mr. Boudreaux! You have been nothing but trouble since you've gotten here!"

"What? I—"

"As the grandson of one of the university's former board members, I had higher expectations! You've done nothing but go against every principle this university stands for. This university serves as an institution for its scholars to lead with integrity and wisdom, something that you clearly lack. I am more disappointed with you out of everyone who is sitting here before me. You're a veteran with aspirations to become a businessman, educator, and coach. You may want to ask yourself, would someone like you, after all these exhibitions of unruly conduct, truly qualify as such? Now, get out of my office!"

The trio exited the office. Paul was flabbergasted at what the dean had said about him in front of his friends. He deemed himself as doing the right thing, getting back at someone who wronged him. Who cares if there wasn't enough proof? Who else would have had any motive to key his car other than Martin, someone who clearly hated his guts and vice versa.

"So much for that," Paul began.

"This is all your fault, Paul," Joel said, halting the walk between them. "The dean's right. You didn't have enough proof, got Greyson and I all fired up, and now we're all in trouble!"

"Oh, so, you've never gotten in trouble before?"

"Not like this! I shouldn't have been called into the office; I didn't even touch the guy! All I'm guilty of is driving on campus and picking up two morons."

"If memory serves me right, I do recall hearing someone say we should go to the medical school to teach him a lesson. Who came up with that idea again?"

"I was only thinking out loud. Nobody had to do it! Besides that, what was with that accusation about you raping someone? That isn't true, is it?"

"That's a damn lie! How could anyone believe that? Why would I? When has Nell or any other woman ever come forward and accused me of such a thing?"

"It's sick, if it's true and you've been invited into our homes and have a daughter too!"

"I said it wasn't true, you dumbass!"

"Chill out, guys," Greyson said. "We shouldn't be at each other's throats like this. Joel, why would you believe that other guy? Paul wouldn't do something like that so whatever that other guy said shouldn't even be relevant. Let's move on."

"Easy for you to say," Joel groaned, swinging his fist into the air. "You two are used to being punks! If the dean found out, other people were squawking about the fight, especially the rape part! What if this hits the press with our names and addresses posted in the paper? I'll be ruined and all due to one stupid mistake!"

"Nobody got arrested or anything, doofus," Greyson spoke. "I need to get my car from the impound lot."

"Are you implying that I should offer either of you a ride?" Joel shrieked. "After everything that's happend? Take the bus and get it yourself! In fact, both of you find your own rides back home!"

Joel kicked his leg into the air before resuming his stroll. Tossing his head back, the man shouted, "God," bringing more attention to himself to confused and curious spectators. Greyson pulled out bits of change from his pants pocket.

"Don't worry about him," Greyson told Paul. "He'll be back to his usual self in a few days. Let's get my car."

After taking the bus to the impound lot, Greyson dropped Paul off at the daycare center to pick up Sharon, and then dropped them off to the garage where the paint and scratches had been repaired. His mood sour, Paul pretended to be cheerful around his daughter throughout the drive home in his vehicle. They returned home and Paul sat on the couch to turn the television on to see if the news would mention anything about the fight. Luckily, there was no mention of the incident on the local news. The news anchors were busy covering news of the US president's impeachment, interviewing people who were excited about an upcoming black film, and the nation's obesity rate.

"I hate that fucking guy," Paul mumbled to himself, reviewing the fight repeatedly in his mind, barely paying attention to what was going on the television set.

He heard the familiar sound of the front door opening and closing followed by the sound of car keys hitting the kitchen counter.

"Paul, I'm back home," Nell's voice called out from the kitchen.

"We're in the living room," Paul responded.

"Okay, getting dinner ready! It's gonna be leftovers."

"Okay, babe!"

Paul rested his head against the back pillows, closing his eyes. *Dinner sounds like a good idea, much better than wasting time thinking about that loser. I got everything that he could possibly want: a beautiful wife, money, a home in an amazing neighborhood, a great kid, good looks, and much more. I bet he went out of his way to find me and Nell. The fool thinks he has a chance to take her away from me. Well, buddy, tonight's gonna be even better knowing I can do things with Nell that he will never get a chance to do.*

Leaning further back, Paul's lips curled into a smile. He began to fall asleep, having a pleasant dream that was partially interrupted by his wife gently calling his name and touching his arm.

"Huh?" Paul asked. "Is dinner ready?"

"No," Nell said, "we need to talk, in private…"

Oh boy, Paul thought, following her into the master bedroom. *What is it this time? She already knows about the car so it should be about something else. I wonder if she's going to talk about her father, nursing school, or about changing her mind about having another kid.*

"While you were sleeping, I called my sister to talk," Nell said. "Claudine told me that Martin called Tyrone to tell him that you and your friends attacked him outside the medical school… Why? Paul, I thought we both agreed to avoid him."

Paul stared ahead, unresponsive.

"So, it's true," Nell uttered. "Paul, they are saying that it's because he's black."

Paul's eyes widened, his mouth almost dropping.

"You're kidding me, right?" he snapped, almost laughing at the notion. "*Because he's black?* Only an idiot would believe that! There's no way! It's because the jerk keyed my car, then called me a *rapist*! He deserved every punch!"

Nell's head drew back quickly. Taking a shaky breath, she asked, "*Rape?* Raped who?"

"He's going around accusing me of raping *you*! That son of a bitch is trying to ruin my life!"

"Well, that part is definitely not true, but Paul, they are saying that you and your friends also attacked a black woman who had to defend herself…"

Paul clenched his fists before releasing them. He released an impatient sneer.

"What motive would any of us have to attack a woman for, black or white? She's the one who swung her purse and attacked us!"

Nell's eyes began to water, her expression pained. "You have almost done so in the past…with me…"

Paul ran his fingers through his hair, feeling almost disoriented upon viewing that his wife was now bawling and avoiding looking his way. *No, no, no!*

"Babe," Paul said, almost begging, "believe me, I've changed a lot because I love you so much. I'll admit to getting my friends involved so we could beat *Martin* up for *ruining my car*, but not because of all this other stuff he's talking about! None of us attacked the woman. She hit us first, several times in fact before I had to take her purse to toss it to the side. Other than that, nothing else was done to her, I swear! I'm sorry and none of this ever should have happened..."

Nell frowned as her posture became rigid. She looked into Paul's eyes as if she were looking into his soul. Nell slowly wrapped her arms around him. Slightly trembling, Paul wrapped his hands around his wife as his eyes went up, looking heavenward.

Thank God, he thought, letting out a huge breath.

"I believe you," Nell told him. "I'm sorry for..."

"I know..."

"Just stay away from him and the medical school...Promise me..."

"Okay, I promise."

"I love you."

"I love you too."

Nell kissed him and walked out of the room. Paul stood there by himself. He let out another huge breath that soon led to an elevated pulse and an edgy, twitchy feeling. His hand curled into a fist. *That son of a bitch is dead meat.*

Chapter 18

That Thursday, it was not surprising that Joel avoided Paul like the plague. Greyson remained neutral and quiet about the incident. Luckily, as far as Paul knew, there were no mentions of what happened the previous day on the news nor in the school media. Paul wanted to return to the medical school and confront Martin alone, but that would only make the jerk look innocent and make Paul appear guilty.

As usual, Paul went to school and picked up his daughter. When they returned home, Paul was surprised to discover his wife's car in the driveway and her sitting on the couch hours before the time she usually returned home. *What's going on? Is she still upset about what happened yesterday? Babe, don't allow this guy to come between us...*

"Hey, baby," Nell greeted their daughter. Her smile wavered at Paul. She turned on the television to a children's program for Sharon and asked Paul to follow her into the master bedroom. *Ugh, what is it this time?* Paul followed her and closed the door behind them. He sat down next to his wife on the edge of the bed. *What's going on?*

"I know we both promised not to go around Martin," Nell said. "But, I didn't go to my campus today...I went to the downtown medical school, not sure if he would be there or not...He wasn't, so I called my sister who gave me Martin's phone number... I was able to contact him, to see if I could clear the air, but he had a lot of disturbing things to say about you... Paul, tell me the truth...At some point, during your first semester at the university, did you have an STD?"

Paul's muscles stiffened involuntarily before he forcibly relaxed them. His skin tingled with discomfort. There was an overwhelming sense of dread that fell upon him. *That low down son of a bitch! Damn! My marriage is over!*

"I told you that I was with other people while we were separated," Paul reminded his wife, scratching at his face. He was unable to meet his wife's gaze.

"He said you have a nickname on campus, *The Walking STD*," Nell told her husband, her voice shaky. "*The Walking STD!* Paul, how many people have you slept with?"

"That's bull crap! Nobody's ever called me that a day in my life! He's making it sound as though I slept with the entire campus!"

"He said at least half!"

"That's pure bullshit! That's not even possible!"

"Tell me the truth, did you ever have an STD or not?"

Paul swung a fist in the air, releasing a strangled cry of frustration. He ran his fingers through his hair, clutching it.

"I did," he confessed, turning pale, "but, I didn't sleep with half the campus!"

"Oh, God, Paul, why?" Nell frowned.

"I'm sorry...I'm sorry, okay! I didn't have sex for a good while, including my entire tour of Vietnam because I kept hoping that I would get a response from you, but hadn't heard anything in years! I thought you moved on, so I tried doing just that! I was depressed, angry, and fucking horny so I shagged a few people! I used condoms, but still got gonorrhea anyway, in my mouth! I was stupid, okay! I got sick, went to the doctor, and they told me I had gonorrhea. It was already going around campus when I got there, but I never thought I'd catch the damned thing! I just wanted to get high, drink, and have a good fuck to help me forget my problems!"

"Why was I never told any of this before?"

"Because I had it treated, long before we got back together. We both were tested before getting married and it came back clear. I didn't think there was a need to say anything! Who would want to confess to anything like that if it had already been treated?"

"Have you slept with anybody else since we've gotten back together?"

"No! Why would I? I've been clean for almost a year and have you. I don't want to sleep with anybody else."

"I went to the clinic and got tested after I got off the phone with Martin. I was angry and disappointed. I wanted to go on your campus, find you, and kill you, but then the doctor told me that I didn't have anything. I wanted to be certain...to be safe."

There was a painful lump in Paul's throat. He began to rub the back of his neck with his hand.

"Angry and disappointed in me, huh? I get it. I would be too. Whenever I think about it, it feels as if I cheated since we technically didn't break up. I'm sorry...I really am...Martin's right, you deserve much, much better than me."

"You didn't cheat, Paul."

"I did and screwed up!"

"We weren't together."

"Nell..."

"But, we're together now, and that's all that matters," Nell sighed. "Things are fine… I think you've been a good husband and father, continue to be that…"

Paul grabbed her hand, desperation in his eyes.

"Nell, I'm sorry…Do you…Do you still love me?" he asked.

"I'll always love you, Paul… We have our moments, but so does every relationship."

Nell embraced him and gave him a reassuring kiss that was returned.

"I love you."

"I love you too."

Paul watched Nell exit the room. He leaned back, falling further onto the softness of the bed. Cupping his hands together, he slid them down his face.

Chapter 19

Greyson continued to flip through the school's paper until he reached the last page. It was Friday and Joel was in better spirits.

"See, there's nothing about us at all," he said tossing the paper to Joel who began scanning through it himself.

"Yeah, but what about the other stuff?" Joel asked.

"C'mon, I'd never do such a thing," Paul sneered. "Name one person whose ever complained about me having sex with them. That geek has been plotting revenge against me since high school and is obviously willing to do whatever it takes to tarnish my name."

"What did you do to him to make him go bananas?" Joel inquired.

"I'll admit I picked on him every once in a while, back then, but what he's really mad over is me marrying the girl he wanted."

"The guy's probably a silver bullet and felt robbed from not hitting third base."

"That's not my fault nor my problem!"

"Imagine someone like him makin' bacon," Greyson laughed repositioning himself and pretending to make a sexual gesture briefly and rolling his eyes to the back of his head. All three guys began to laugh.

"That would be him alone with his Johnson," Paul laughed.

"He probably jerks off to the periodic table," Greyson chuckled. "Or says something stupid like E=mc sssqqquuuuaaarrreee when he gets off."

"Shut up," Joel laughed, grabbing his sides, almost slipping off the bench.

Greyson accidentally farted, resulting in Paul and Joel chuckling even harder as they moved away from him. Paul covered his nose with his hand while Joel tucked his own nose underneath his shirt.

"Greyson cut the cheese," Joel laughed.

"You're nasty, man," Paul added. "That one sounded like it's gonna leave skid marks!"

"Ugh, what did you eat for lunch, it stinks!"

Margo, Laura, and Clair approached them. Margo began to gag. Laura's face became pinched, and Clair began to fan at the air.

"Gross," Margo complained. "What's that horrible smell? Did someone fart?"

"Grow up," Clair told the guys.

"Paul, is everything okay with Nell and Sharon?" Laura asked. "I didn't mean to upset your little girl after she heard about the kittens."

"It's no big deal," Paul assured her. "Sharon can be very passionate about animals. Nell and I have been taking her to the pet store to visit the animals there, but we want to make sure she knows more about them first before we get her first pet."

"I have one kitten left," Laura said. "She can have it if it's okay with your wife. Its three months old and a male."

"Thanks, when would be a good time to pick him up?"

"Anytime, I guess. I have a few supplies I can give to get you started until you get more."

"Wow, that's awesome! Thanks! Sharon'll be so excited! We'll drop by Friday to pick him up."

"Good, I'm glad he'll be going to a good home."

Paul said his goodbyes and left the group. He was relieved that he did not see any new damage to his vehicle nor saw his rival along the highway while driving to pick up his little girl. They went to the pet store to purchase pet supplies. Paul informed Sharon that they were getting the treats for a special new friend, exciting the little girl.

I hope Nell will be okay with this. This is a little sudden. Soon, they left the store and returned home. Paul turned on the television set and sat down on the couch. Sharon snuggled next to him, watching the daily children's program. Paul kissed his daughter's forehead, grateful for the moment.

"I'll pick Sharon up after my classes are done," Paul said. *"She's not that far from my school, and…it will be nice, not going home to an empty place…"*

A cereal commercial was featured on the television. Together, Paul and Sharon began to sing along to the commercial. Shortly, Nell arrived home, and Paul left the living room to join his wife in the kitchen.

"Hey, honey," Paul greeted her exchanging a kiss.

"Hey, handsome," Nell replied. "How were your classes?"

"Classes are good! Things are slowly getting back to normal…So, Laura is giving Sharon a kitten. Is it okay to pick him up tomorrow? I think it would be fine. I've been helping her with learning how to take care of a family pet each afternoon. She's been practicing with her stuffed animals, so I think that she will take having a new pet seriously."

"Sure, I think Sharon knows more about kittens than she did before."

"And, you haven't forgotten about the football gathering the weekend after I come home from the armory, right?

"Nope, I already know you want hot dogs, chicken wings, chips, pizza, and a thousand other things."

"And you for myself," Paul added with a wink.

Nell began to giggle.

"Hey, don't forget to bring some friends over from the other school," Paul said. "We could also invite a few neighbors over like the Reeves since their daughter is always kind enough to babysit."

"We might run out of room inviting all these people over!"

"This house is big! There's plenty of room! We can also make good use of the grill! I'll get out the portable television and some of us can watch or listen to the game outside."

Paul began to utter a melody, dancing steadily towards his wife. Taking her hand, he gave her a twirl, and a dip.

"Get out of the kitchen, Casanova," Nell laughed, as she pulled back upright.

"Nope, I'm too busy having fun right here," Paul replied.

Knock! Knock!

Paul turned towards the front door.

"Expecting any company, babe?" he asked.

"No," Nell answered.

Paul opened the front door to see a familiar face. It was their teenage neighbor, Ginger Reeves. Her brown hair was pulled into a single ponytail. Her brown eyes were kind, and she was wearing a light blue dress and brown wedged shoes.

Paul wondered why the teen was there, until she brought forth a small white envelope in her hands, handing it to him.

"Hi, Ginger, what's this?" Paul asked, taking the envelope.

"I don't know, Mr. Boudreaux," Ginger said. "My mother told me to give this to you. She said that earlier today, she saw a black woman in front of your home and asked the woman who she was, but the woman wouldn't say. She gave my mother this envelope and asked her to give it to you. Were you expecting it?"

"No, but let me take a look," Paul said, tearing the side of the envelope open and peeking inside. Inside it contained money, making him do a double take. *What on Earth is this for?* He looked to see if there was a message included, but there was nothing more inside. "Thanks, Ginger. How's school going?"

"Alright," Ginger replied. "In Home Economics, the class was learning how to make aprons. I thought mine was fine until I realized that I sewed the neck strap wrong. Luckily, Mrs. Finley was understanding and didn't take off too many points for the assignment. I'll be sure not to make the same mistake twice."

"That's nice of her. Do you have plans on making more aprons in the future?"

"I don't know. Maybe, I will, if that means it'll help me earn enough money to save up for my own car. I'm halfway there!"

"Awesome, you can count on us purchasing a few! Also, Nell and I will be needing a babysitter soon. So, that'll help even further."

"Neat!"

"Great, I'll let you and your folks know when," Paul went back inside the house. He saw that Nell was humming to herself in the kitchen, resuming her cooking.

A black woman, Paul thought. *Could it be someone that Nell knows? Why would the person be here to leave me money? Do I know this individual? How does this person know where I live? Could it be Tracy or Mrs. Ann? Why would they do this?*

"Honey," Paul said, "were any of your friends here earlier today and left me something with the Reeves?"

"No," Nell told him. "Not that I know of. Nobody said anything to me during class and it's not my turn to host the study group. We're all going to Sandra's next week. Was it a man or a woman?"

"Ginger said it was a woman," Paul's voice trailed, looking inward. *A woman...* Turning almost pale, he soon realized what he needed to do.

Chapter 20

His eyes cold, Paul entered the room. Today, he was breaking yet another promise to himself: to not skip class. Nevertheless, it was necessary to be done, for him, his marriage, and his sanity. Being there again brought back feelings of anxiety, embarrassment, and disgust. It didn't matter why he was there; all eyes were on him from everyone who was present.

There were ten people sitting in the lobby that day, scattered in different seats. Paul didn't want to know why each was there, nor did he care to share why he was there himself. He didn't know the name of the person that he was searching. He knew what she looked like, and there she was on the other side of the receptionist's window with a clipboard in her hand. She didn't notice Paul, retreating out of the room through a back door.

Paul approached the window.

"Excuse me," he said to the receptionist, "who was that woman with the clipboard that just left?"

"Are you referring to Dr. Washington?"

"I think so," Paul said. "I need to speak to her."

"She's with a patient right now, but I will let her know that you are here. May I have your name?"

After Paul gave the receptionist his name, he waited in the lobby. He eyed the exit, wishing he never had to return to the facility. He recollected how humiliating it was to be there the first time and discover why his throat had been sore, why he had difficulty swallowing, why he had redness in his throat, and why he had swollen lymph nodes that wouldn't go away.

Minutes later, the door separating the lobby from a backroom opened and a man and woman walked out. The woman, Dr. Washington, stood at the door with a clipboard. Her eyes met Paul's causing his chest to develop a sharp pain. *So, it was her! She's the person who was there with Martin the day we had the fight in the parking lot and ...the day I received treatment!*

Chapter 21

"Hey, aren't you the woman who was with Martin in the parking lot a few days ago?" Paul asked, sitting in the outpatient room.

Dr. Washington closed the door, taking a seat near him.

"Yes," she answered. "I was… What brings you back to the clinic today?"

A tightness in Paul's expression was met with a direct stare that lacked warmth.

"You're the one behind everything, aren't you?" Paul stated, using a carefully controlled tone. "The scratches in my vehicle, my wife finding out about the gonorrhea, and the envelope. Did Martin put you up to this?"

"No, he did not," Dr. Washington replied, in a matter-of-fact voice. "In fact, Martin knew nothing about the car because I was the one who keyed it. The envelope I left should have been more than enough to cover the repairs, so why are you here?"

"Because I want to figure out why you're doing all this! What have I ever done to you personally?" Paul's body temperature began to rise. His fingers began to retract, turning claw-like before slowly forming into balled fist that began to shake. He took a deep breath to calm himself.

"Simple," Dr. Washington answered. "Because I hate you, for what you did to my man. Martin and I have been seeing each other for about three years and I've always heard terrible stories about how you and those other white folks went around that high school terrorizing the black students… Martin told me how you and those other h****** used to have fun beating him up every other day, forcing him to eat toilet paper, spitting in his food, shoving him into lockers, knocking his books out his hands, and so much more. Get all mad with me all you like, but what about low down people such as yourself who think it's perfectly fine to terrorize another human being for going to school to better themselves?"

"You're not the police, jury, nor judge! That gives you no right to try to ruin my life or my things! All of that was years ago! I was a different person then!"

"Are you? You and your friends had no problems singling him out to beat him up in the parking lot."

"That's because I thought it was him who scratched my car! Nobody else had any motive that I could think of back then!"

"Oh yeah," Dr. Washinton scoffed, "so much for that. Martin's been going out of his way to avoid you on campus! There are plenty of people who don't like you."

"How do you figure? Why is your boyfriend even on this campus out of any place he could have gone in the world? He's still jealous about me being with my wife, I bet!"

"Wrong, Martin applied and got a full scholarship to the university, with the help of his science teacher from Wood Oak High School. She was one of the few white folks who believed in him and his future. He was at the university before you came. Martin never mentioned anything about you until the day he discovered that you both were going to the same university and told me what he went through. He wanted nothing to do with you, and yet every once in a blue moon, he'd spot you around campus drunk, high, or making out with some nasty women. Since gonorrhea was spreading on campus, it wasn't surprising that you had to eventually come to the clinic! I remember the day I was able to put your name and face together…I had to have my faith in God tested more than ever because I didn't even want to treat you because you deserved it all! It took everything I had not to walk back into the room, lie, say you were fine, and that it should clear up in a few days. Only my fear of God helped you that day."

Paul's jaw became set. He dug his fingers into his chair.

"I told Martin," Dr. Washington continued, "hoping it would make him happy to know how far you've fallen, but he felt sorry instead. That surprised me, but he never laughed or joked about it. I know plenty of people who would have. Yeah, I keyed your car and it felt good to show that you couldn't get away with everything. But then, Nell called and that made me wonder if she was trying to reconnect with Martin, but he said they only talked about the fight, and he warned her about being with someone as disgusting as you for her own good."

"You two are something else," Paul said. "That information was supposed to remain confidential! I could have you both fired and lose your medical licenses!"

"What proof would you have that I've done anything? As far as I am concerned, you could be another disgruntled patient that may need to seek treatment in a mental asylum."

"I have connections within the university at the top administrative levels that are more than qualified to help pull your license preventing you from practicing medicine. Not only that, but you will be deemed ineligible from most walks of life if you try to seek employment elsewhere. Maybe you might be set up and thrown in prison. Your money could mysteriously disappear overnight. Maybe you or some close member of your family disappears never to be seen again. Maybe one day you'll wake up to find yourself buried underground where nobody can save you. We can go back and forth, but I can assure you that if you're willing to take the chance to see if I'm bluffing or not, you're as good as gone and will wish that you were right next to me in the asylum that you're wanting to put me in."

Dr. Washington sneered at Paul.

"Anyway, I'm glad we've come to an understanding and that things have been resolved," Paul continued. "Should there be more concerns, I will take them on myself, not my wife. I trust that there will no longer be any interference on your part nor Martin's, should you both know what's in store should there be a change."

Paul rose from his chair, keeping an equal intense stare at the doctor as he exited the room and out the clinic. As the sun shined, he closed his eyes and tossed his head back. He covered his eyes with his hands, inhaled, and exhaled. He uncovered his eyes, regaining his composure.

He had mixed feelings about Martin. So, the man was innocent as far as the car was concerned, but did he have to tell Nell about the STD? It was treated, but what if it wasn't? What would things have been like then? Would their lives be different? Either way, Paul was grateful that he did not pass the disease to his wife. *I will not allow my past to ruin what I have going on today or in the future. I will do better and continue to do so. People like Dr. Washington may see me as a monster, but I will not allow people like her to deter me from my goals. I have changed for the better and can still be a good person.*

Chapter 22

The following Friday, Paul and his friends were in the union eating lunch. He was still in a bitter mood about Dr. Washington but kept it to himself. He had other concerns such as missing his family to fulfill his duties at the armory.

The ham and Swiss cheese sandwich that Paul was eating tasted surprisingly good, making his tastebuds crave a second. *I got to stop eating so much, but darn, this sandwich, mmm!*

Greyson sat across from Paul reading an article about an illegal gambling operation that had taken place an hour away from the university. The police had arrested fifty people for horse betting, playing blackjack, having a roulette wheel, and other games. That reminded Paul of the stories he had heard about his uncles and their gambling addictions. *What was so good about gambling anyway when it was possible to lose lots of assets within a matter of minutes?* They had lost their fortunes and homes, angry at others but themselves.

"How much do you owe in loans?" Margo asked Clair.

"Not much," Clair stated. "I'm hoping that most of it will be paid off before I graduate. But inflation isn't helping much… What do you think, Cindy?"

"Everything's fine," Cindy responded. For the last few months, she had been absent from the group, but showed up that day. "Things couldn't be better!"

Paul knew that was a lie. The woman had loans up to her eyeballs, only revealing how bad it was to him and Margo. Cindy had outstanding credit cards and a car loan. It appeared that money slipped from her hands like water falling from a fishnet. In the past, Paul had attempted to assist her financially, in which Cindy had been grateful, but even when one debt was paid in full, there was another to take its place.

"Did you sell any artwork at the last show?" Laura asked.

"No," Cindy replied, a heavy sigh, "but it would have been nice if I did. I plan on putting my work in an art show downtown. The Chlorophyll Gallery is gathering works of art done by women for its upcoming show and I'll put the same pieces from the Crimson Gallery in."

"Everyone's going, of course," Laura told her, with the others in the group nodding.

"Right on!"

"We'll be there!"

"I'm also looking forward to going to Paul's place," Clair stated.

"Are we doing this potluck style?" Joel asked.

"No," Paul answered, "all the food'll be there. Just bring your appetites."

"Hey, that won't be too much cooking for Nell, will it?" Margo asked.

"I'll be helping her," Paul said. "I've helped out at plenty of parties before. My folks used to have guests every other weekend back at the old house."

"This is football," Greyson contested. "You won't be paying attention to the food! It'll be as good as burnt if Nell is depending on you to help."

"We'll all bring something anyway," Laura said. "That way Paul can watch the game and we can get to know his wife better. Is she going invite people from her school as well?"

"Sure," Paul said. "It'll probably be the same folks from her study group. They're all pretty much like us, coming from all walks of life."

"How's your daughter doing?" Clair asked.

"Great! Sharon's excited to be getting one of Laura's kittens later today."

"How old is she again? Three?"

"No, she's four."

"Wow, like Jacob," Laura added. "You and Nell had Sharon pretty early. I can't imagine being a parent at eighteen! I can barely afford to take care of myself, much less with a kid."

"Nell hit the jackpot with Paul," Clair giggled. "Paul is so in love! His face always lights up whenever he talks about her. I don't think I've ever seen him be so happy in a relationship."

Cindy's smile slowly dissipated. There was a sharp bump heard from underneath the table.

"Ow," Clair cried out, grimacing. She turned to Margo, who gave her a harsh look that implied for her to shut up.

"I'm still hungry," Greyson grumbled, eating the last bit of his sandwich.

"How?" Laura exclaimed. "You ate three sandwiches already! Stop being greedy!"

"They were small," Greyson complained motioning his hands to make his fingers look like small squares. "I'm a grown man and these sandwiches aren't enough to feed the ants."

"Nah, it's greed," Joel countered.

"Bug off!"

Everyone at the table laughed. Paul balled up his wrapper and walked to the trashcan to discard it. Greyson left the group to purchase another sandwich. Margo excused herself from the table, following Paul to the other end of the deli.

"Hey, Paul," she whispered. "I was thinking, it won't be an issue having Cindy go to your place that weekend, will it?"

"I hope not, why?"

"It's obvious that she still isn't over the breakup."

"Gary didn't sound like a good guy in the first place. Those two should have broken up a long time ago."

"Get real! It was all a lie! There is no Gary! Cindy only made him up as a ploy to get back together with you. He's never shown up for any of us to meet him nor has Cindy ever shown anyone a picture! He doesn't exist! Cindy misses you! She called me and Laura the other day and told us! I told her she needs to be considerate and think of other people, not just herself! She doesn't care and wants to get back together!"

"No way," Paul spoke, his limbs tingling with fatigue. "I'm tired of all the lies! I can't get back together with Cindy! I'm married! All Cindy and I ever did was break up and get back together! I don't need nor want that anymore! My family's important to me...I have them to think about!"

"I told her that so many times!"

"Then keep telling her because it's obvious that she won't listen to me!"

"She won't listen to me either!"

Paul scraped a hand over his face, pinching his lips thin.

"Is that why she's starting to come back around again? Because she thinks she can weasel her way back in? No way! I'm sick of this crap!"

The young man went back to the table where the rest of his friends sat. He asked Cindy to follow him to speak to her in private. He was done. That chapter in his past was over whether Cindy accepted it or not.

"I'm not trying to single you out," Paul said, "but I don't think it would be a good idea for you to come watch the game at my house. I heard a few things…and I'm not interested in reliving the past. It's not about only me anymore. I have a wife and little girl to think about. We can still be friends and keep things casual, but at a distance. There will be no getting back together between us."

Cindy's eyes began to brim with tears. She rushed back to the table, grabbed her belongings, and left the group.

"Hey, where's Cindy heading off to?" Greyson asked, stuffing his face with one of the egg salad sandwiches that he had purchased. He placed the sandwich between his teeth with one brown bag in his hand and his wallet in the other. He attempted to put his wallet in his pants pocket, almost dropping his bag clumsily. He walked back to the table, placing the bag on top and sitting down.

"It's nothing," Paul said, taking a seat, and staring ahead to anywhere past their concerned faces.

"I'm going to go and check on her," Laura said, leaving the table. Clair and Margo followed.

"What's the deal," Joel inquired. "All the girls left after Cindy. Was she crying? I wonder what happened this time."

"Cindy wants to get back together *again*," Paul spoke in an unsteady voice.

Greyson gasped, nearly choking on his sandwich. He began to beat his chest, coughing.

"Really," Greyson gasped, his eyes bulging and a smirk forming. "How is that going to work out now that you are married?"

"Far out," Joel exclaimed, grinning with a chuckle. "Cindy's letting nothing stand in her way, no other woman, no kids, not even a marriage! She's got guts!"

"I dig it," Greyson said smiling towards the sky with a dreamy look upon his face. "I wish it were me. A woman fighting to not be forgotten and left behind. She's hooked line and sinker to Paul's Johnson."

"It may sound cool, but it's not," Paul argued. "It took years to get Nell back. Last thing I need to happen is for an ex-girlfriend to ruin things. Cindy already knows I'm not interested. This has got to stop!"

"Be honest, if you weren't married and didn't have a kid and Cindy didn't have a kid, would you choose her or Nell?" Greyson inquired.

"Nell, duh," Paul replied.

"Whose better in bed?"

"That's none of your business, you skuzz!"

"So, Cindy then!"

"I didn't say that!"

"Then, Nell!"

"Shut up, you dumbass!"

Greyson continued to laugh, almost spitting out parts of his meal. Joel kneeled over in his chair, grabbing his sides, tears forming while he chuckled. Paul rested his chin in the palm of his hand, his face becoming red. He stared angrily at his friends.

"I knew this would happen," Joel confessed. "Remember the first semester when everyone was still getting to know each other, and Cindy begged all the girls to not say anything about Jacob because she really liked Paul? When Margo told me Cindy's secret, I told her Paul wasn't going to like that at all and needed to tell him. She made a mess of things."

"There's more to it than her simply being a single mom," Paul said. "I told her and all the other girls that I didn't want anything serious since day one. I was still trying to get over my own baggage and didn't want anyone to become too attached to anybody."

"Yeah, you've really scaled back since then! Plus, most guys our age don't want to be bothered. We want to have fun, not help junior with his homework."

"Get real! What kind of homework is a four-year-old gonna have other than a coloring page at the least? Jacob's not that bad. He's full of energy, likes to play at the playground, and look at bugs."

"True, but that kid throws a temper tantrum whenever he doesn't get his way! Who wants to deal with that?"

"Most four-year-olds do, including Sharon. You just got to teach them to have patience and persevere. Even adults have problems with that apparently."

"Whatever happens, don't make bacon with Cindy without a condom," Greyson chimed in. "She'll probably try to get pregnant on purpose, out of desperation, if a marriage isn't stopping her."

"Listen, Cindy is a sweet girl, but I'm not cheating on my wife."

"I thought of something," Joel added. "Maybe love has nothing to do with the situation at all. It could be dollar signs! Most girls on campus are looking for some rich fool to marry or shag to have an easy lavish lifestyle.

Isn't Cindy poor? She never would have gotten into this university without that scholarship. I bet she thought she hit the jackpot by getting accepted here!"

"Bug off Cindy, guys," Paul said, pressing a hand against his forehead. "Stop looking down on her because she's a single mother with feelings and not as wealthy as most people on campus. Like Dean Kelly said, without our families, we probably wouldn't be on this campus ourselves. At least someone saw talent within Cindy to permit her to earn her spot at the university."

Paul looked down at his watch. It was 1:30 pm and he was beginning to develop a headache.

"I'm gonna head to class," he spoke. "I'll catch everyone later."

Chapter 23

"How was school?"

"Fine," Paul replied. "Things are going well. I'm making sure that my grades are good and listening to the teachers…but I'm still bummed about your health. I…I wish I could stay to be here with you…"

"Don't worry about me; it's part of getting old," Abraham coughed. "It's only inevitable to die…Soon, it will be my turn, and one day it will be yours, but hopefully not for a long time…If there is anything I could wish for, for not myself, but for you, is for you to live a life without regrets. That's the best way to live life, even if others perceive it as wrong."

"Are you regretting something? What was it?"

*"Taking the life of my son, Philip… Sometimes, I see him waiting for me at the foot of the bed, alongside the faces of all the people I killed, including those dirty n*****s. They're all waiting, to see if they can drag me to Hell with them. My own son…He joined them…He joined them against his own father."*

"You're not going to Hell, Grandfather," Paul answered giving a sidelong glance while keeping his head still.

*"Then why is that n***** at my door?" the elder demanded pointing to the entrance of the room.*

Paul looked at the door, seeing nothing. He wanted to leave, hating the slow deterioration that was happening before his eyes. He had hoped that by some miracle that the elderly man would get better, but now he was seeing things, things that nobody else could see for the last few days.

"There's nobody there," Paul told him.

"He is! He's right there!"

The nurse rushed into the room. She began to sedate Abraham, who kept pointing and shouting. Paul rushed outside the room, entering the men's restroom. Leaning heavily over the dry sink, Paul began to shiver, clutching to the sink's frame. He looked around him, searching for the person that his grandfather was seeing. Paul was alone, not seeing anyone.

"How'd things go at the hospital?" Nell asked later that day.

"Not so good," Paul responded. "My grandfather… he's…he's been seeing things…things that aren't there. It was scary, like he really believes what he is seeing…ghosts and going to Hell…He said that one day it'll be my turn… I don't want to go to Hell…"

"Good people don't go to Hell," Nell told him.

"I don't think I'm a good person, not after what I've done to you…and Martin…"

"You apologized in your own way and regretted your prior actions."

"Isn't life about having no regrets?"

"That would be nice, but not too realistic…How would anyone learn without a few?"

"But that still doesn't make someone a good person. What if I keep doing things that I'll regret later, intentional, or unintentional?"

"It's okay to forgive yourself, if that's what you're asking."

"I'm not sure… Nell, have you ever thought about dying?"

"Sometimes, especially at funerals or after visiting gravesites. I like to think, that they are going home to a happy place…A place where there is no suffering and everyone gets along no matter who they are."

"A happy place, huh…Let's make a deal, to go to that happy place together when we die."

"Why wait until we die? Why not make the lives we are living now a happy place?"

"Good point! Hey… sorry for being a downer as of late… I, uh, try not to let things get the better of me… There have been times where I …I …would drink a lot, to escape … to not care about anything. I still do."

"Instead of drinking when times get hard, how about we can talk… about anything."

"Nobody wants to hear someone be negative all the time."

"You're not. You're usually happy-go-lucky most of the time."

"True, but, I don't want to look weak. Men aren't supposed to be all emotional. Crying and feeling down is usually for girls."

"It's not. It's okay to feel sad about things, even if you are a guy. Think about it… After drinking, those problems will still be there, so why do it?"

"I've been doing it since I was thirteen."

"Really? That young? Do you plan on stopping?"

"I don't know. Maybe not."

"Well… I wish you didn't feel like you had to. What if something bad happens to you?"

"Nothing's happened so far."

"Or yet, you mean…Paul, I'm glad you're opening more about yourself, but when times get really difficult, I *want you to know that I'm here to help. I love you, allow for me to be there for you."*

"How can someone like you help me? Most people here hate people like you, but you can help solve all my problems?"

"But a bottle can? At least I can talk back and love you. Yes, I know people hate me. They show me that every day with how they act, but I don't have to be ignorant and downright evil like them because I know who and what kind of person I am. No, I can't solve all your problems, but I must be doing something for you to have revealed so much about yourself."

Nell's face softened. Paul lowered his head and Nell pressed her forehead against his before leaning further in to embrace him.

"Aren't you afraid of what I could become," Paul asked.

"I don't know what person you'll become in the future, but I love the person you are now."

"I love you too..."

I think, I'll be an even better person to love, in this happy place I'm seeing because of you.

After school, Paul took Sharon over to Laura's apartment to pick up the kitten. The kitten was a small black and white tuxedo cat that Sharon decided to name Alex. Excited, the little girl could hardly contain herself in the car for the drive home, begging her father to hold the pet.

"We're almost home, babydoll," Paul stated, pulling into the driveway and parking the vehicle. He helped both Sharon and the kitten into the home where he immediately released the new pet from the carrier. The cat began to stretch before making its way out. Sharon began to pet Alex, bringing joy to Paul's heart. He sat down with them on the floor, watching his little girl crawl on the floor with Alex. A smile making its way upon his face, Paul decided to do the same, adding some toys they had gotten from the pet store onto the floor.

"I'm gonna be a kitty too," Sharon giggled, imitating the stretching the cat did and crawling across the floor.

Paul rolled one of the balls across the floor. Alex began to run after it. Thirty minutes later, Nell returned home where Paul and Sharon introduced her to Alex, the new addition to their happy place.

Chapter 24
Nell

That weekend, Paul left to fulfill his military duties at the armory. Sharon and Alex stayed at home under the supervision of their neighbor, Ginger, while Nell visited the public library to study and complete the assignments for her classes.

The library was Nell's second home. Thanks to Paul picking up Sharon in the afternoons, she was able to visit.

I wonder what it'll be like, having people from both schools together at home, Nell thought. *The people from Paul's school seemed to be okay. They're much different than his friends from Wood Oak. Everyone from my school likes him and Sharon. So, maybe things will be fine. Paul gave me a long list of food items, but said everyone could still bring food if they wanted... I better plan on getting lots of foil for the to go plates...*

Nell began to collect the library books into her arms. One by one, she placed them back on the shelves where they were stored. The library had books that seemed to be much more detailed than the books assigned to her in her classes, making her wonder why the newer books did not contain essential information. As much as she wanted to take the extra books home, she could barely keep up with the ones she already checked out, barely able to recall their due dates by a day or two.

The blurs began to slowly form into clearer shapes of trees and buildings. The bus arrived at its destination with the driver opening its doors. Three of its passengers exited, including Nell who had begun to bite into a piece of bread she had purchased earlier that day to alleviate the hunger pangs. She prayed for Paul to get her letter soon while he was still within the walls of the Marine Corps Recruit Depot. She wasn't allowed near nor on the facility. She had no choice but to wait for him, with the money that was beginning to quickly deplete right before her eyes.

For the last few days, Nell had been staying at a hotel. It was eerie being alone in an unknown area without her family who she left in Illinois. Her father had given her a choice, to stay with her family or be with Paul. She had made her decision, but did Paul know that she was so close? She did not have a telephone number to call him, only a pencil and a piece of paper that she had obtained from one of the young hotel maids. Nell gave her letter to the hotel manager who stated that he would try to find a way to get it to Paul. It was not long after and without a response, the money was down to the last bits of change.

I can't go back home, Nell thought opening the door to the hotel's office. Dad will never let me live this down. He'll call me a fool again for getting pregnant and not finishing school...He doesn't understand anything! If he can love my mom, why can't I love Paul?

"Hi there, Nell," the hotel manager said from behind the front desk. "Did you hear back from the young man yet?"

"No, not yet," Nell said, her mouth getting dry. "I can't afford to stay another night. Is there any work I could do to earn an extra stay?"

"For how long?"

"I don't know. I was hoping to hear back from my boyfriend by now, but there still hasn't been a response."

"I wish I could do more to help, but I've never been on the base myself. All I could do was ask a friend from the

post office to mail it off with the exact address. He told me that there's this saying that nobody ever sees anyone leave on or off the base until visiting day. That's the day before the recruits graduate, which is a few days from now. If your boyfriend knows you're coming a week before, he can put your name on a list to get on the base before they leave, which would be the day after graduation...I've been praying that your boyfriend writes back, but I hate to admit that there have been a few women that came here, hoping to reconnect with the men on the base only to find out that they've moved on, leaving them behind."

Trying not to let the words sink in, a pain formed in Nell's throat. Paul would never do that to me...He promised...Not after everything we've been through together... He wrote that he wanted me back...

"Tell ya what, the Rose Baptist Church isn't too far from here. They have a small program where they offer temporary housing for women and single mothers."

The manager wrote down the address and gave it to Nell.

After Nell returned home, she thanked and paid Ginger for watching Sharon. Sharon was sitting near the coffee table where she was coloring a picture of a giraffe with a yellow crayon. Alex was sleeping on the loveseat.

"Hey, baby," Nell greeted the little girl who immediately stopped to rise to her feet.

"Mommy," Sharon exclaimed, embracing her mother with a wide smile. She returned to the table and gave her mother the picture she had been coloring. It had yellow and brown scribbles.

"Wow, that's pretty," Nell said. "It's going right on the refrigerator!"

She and Sharon entered the kitchen where Nell placed the picture on the refrigerator with a letter G magnet. There were other letter magnets scattered on the refrigerator. Often, Nell and Paul would review each letter with Sharon, sometimes adding two or three together, sounding them out. Nell dragged a letter closer to Sharon.

"S," Sharon giggled.

"S as in Sharon," Nell smiled, playfully pressing a finger on top of her daughter's nose. She moved another letter nearby. "What letter is this?"

"P!"

"What about this one?"

"G!"

Nell moved another letter closer to the letter G.

"Ok, sound it out," she told the little girl.

"Gee-oh."

"Sound it out. Guh-oh."

"Guh...ow?"

"Guh-oh."

"Guh-oh."

"Go."

"Go!"

"Sister Martha, this is Sister Nell," a middle-aged black woman named Mrs. Jackson said to an elderly black woman who was dozing in and out of sleep. Mrs. Jackson continued the tour of the Rose Baptist Church, introducing Nell to the people they came across. Mrs. Jackson was a black woman with black and grey hair, dark brown eyes.

She was well dressed in a dark blue dress and high heels. Nell was careful not to tell the woman too much about herself. She had already asked too many questions such as: who are your kinfolks, what brings you here, how old are you, why aren't you at home with your parents?

As much as Nell hated the questions, she simply replied that she didn't want to say, making the woman even more suspicious, until she confessed that her parents knew about her departure from home. Mrs. Jackson's eyes peered down at Nell's protruding belly with disagreeable judgement.

"Reverend Davis and Deacon Seymore, this is Sister Nell," Mrs. Jackson said to the two men who were walking opposite of them in the hallway. "She's new. She'll be staying with us for a bit."

"Welcome, Sister Nell," Reverend Davis said, giving her a firm handshake. "Do you sing?"

"Not really," Nell responded, biting down on her bottom lip.

"Well, the choir will be having practice soon, if you'd like to join us," the reverend smiled, continuing his walk with Deacon Seymore. The reverend was elderly with a bald head, dark brown skin, dark brown eyes, and black clothing.

Deacon Seymore was in his late fifties with light brown skin and dark brown eyes. He dressed well in a brown jacket, yellow shirt, brown pants, and black shoes. He simply nodded Nell's way, following the reverend without uttering a word.

Mrs. Jackson showed Nell the dining hall where the church had their receptions, the room where Bible study took place, a nursery, offices, restrooms, and finally a section where the women and children were kept.

Nell was given a small room with a bed, lamp, and table where a Bible was placed. There was no window or closet area. It was simply a place to rest her head. Nell was given the task of cleaning the kitchen, cleaning the Bible study room after Wednesday's prayer meetings and Sunday's services, and assisting as needed.

Mrs. Jackson left Nell in the room she had been given. There was no television, other books, or anything to keep herself occupied, other than reading the Bible. All that was happening was the choir practice that the reverend had mentioned. It was much too early to be sleeping, leaving her no choice but to revisit the rooms where her chores were to be performed. Everything was tidy, not requiring much effort.

Soon, Nell heard a piano playing. It was a cheerful tune followed by the sound of voices singing. Nell opened the door to see two rows of people singing, a young choir director in his late twenties at the piano, directing them with his nods and telling brown eyes. He was well dressed in a dark blue shirt, black pants, and shiny, polished black shoes. He had a handsome smile, a medium sized afro, and glasses. He nodded Nell's way, continuing to play the piano with the quick movements of his fingers.

Nell sat down in one of the pews at the back of the church, until the music stopped.

"Come on up and join us, sister," the choir director called out with a wide grin.

Nell swallowed hard. She didn't want to sing. She only wanted to listen to the music, but was she allowed to say no? The director extended his arm, beckoning for her to join the rest of the choir who had begun to become quieter.

"What's your name?" one of the young women in the choir asked. "I've never seen you around here before."

"It's Nell," Nell said, clearing her throat. "Nell Jefferson…"

"What you say?" the woman asked, her voice loud and clear.

"Nell," Nell repeated, her voice louder.

"Alright, Sister Nell. I'm Elsie Gaines. You gonna sing with us?"

"I don't really sing…"

"Everyone sings in God's house," the woman waved for Nell to join her at her side.

Reluctantly, Nell complied, and the director began a new song with the choir singing once more. Nell was not familiar with the new song that they were singing, but it was even more captivating than the previous one. The choir began to sway side to side with the music, clapping their hands. The woman next to Nell, began to sing a solo part to the song, her voice had spunk and her added movements had an attitude that made Nell smile, almost releasing a slight chuckle.

The woman looked to be in her late twenties. She had dark brown skin, large dark brown eyes, and a short afro. She was thin and wore a yellow blouse, green dress, and brown shoes.

After the choir had its practice, the choir director, who Nell soon learned was named Frederick Harris, began asking her just as many questions as Mrs. Jackson. There was the usual, where are you from, what brings you to South Carolina, and much more. Nell hated all the questioning that was going on. It seemed as if everyone wanted to be in her business, probably to gossip to their friends or family later.

"You're originally from Louisiana?" Elsie exclaimed. "I've always wanted to go down to New Orleans and see the French Quarter!"

"They make a mean seafood gumbo in the French Quarter," Frederick added. "Three years ago, the choir went to New Orleans for a music festival. We had so much fun! I'm making plans for us returning next year."

"If Nell sticks around, she can join us," Elsie added.

Frederick nodded in agreement.

"That was a good practice," he said. "I would stay longer, but I have to head to the college to teach my class."

"You're a college professor?" Nell asked.

"Yep, I teach music classes at the community college ten miles away from here," Frederick said. "It was nice having you sing with us today, Sister Nell. We'd love to have you be with us this Sunday during church service."

Nell forced a smile. Her singing in front of other people? She barely made it during the practice, much less in front of other strangers!

"How far along are you?" Elsie inquired, gawking at Nell's belly.

"Seven months," Nell answered.

"You married? I don't see a ring on your finger."

Nell didn't want to respond, but she did want to tell Elsie to shut up. Was she married herself? Elsie didn't have a ring on her finger either! Nell may not have had a wedding band, but she still had Paul's high school ring hanging from her necklace. It was something!

"Stop asking her all those personal questions," Frederick told Elsie.

Thank you, Nell thought. At least someone has some manners!

"You asked questions," Elsie argued, "but it's not okay for me to ask any?"

"I didn't ask that."

"But probably thought about it, huh?"

"I'm getting married," Nell said, hoping that one day the words would be true. They had to be! Paul would want to. They talked so many times about being together to raise their child.

Elsie hushed, rolling her eyes. The remainder of the choir left for the day, with Frederick departing with them. Sadly, all that remained was Nell and Elsie, someone who left a bitter taste in Nell's mouth. Not wanting to be bothered with the woman anymore, Nell headed to the restroom. Later, she left to return to her room, but was surprised to see Elsie entering the same hallway, carrying a baby in her own arms.

Chapter 25

"Hold still," Nell instructed Sharon, brushing the little girl's hair, and braiding it into two braids. Doing Sharon's hair wasn't too bad, but the little girl was known to be tender headed. Heck, Nell's own mother used to complain about how Nell and Claudine were tender headed too, yelping as she would brush between strands that needed to be untangled. "Ok, finished!"

The task completed; Sharon began to play with Alex who dashed away, entering the kitchen to jump on the counter, and jumping once more to the top of the refrigerator. He rolled to his side to peer down at the little girl.

Rrriiinnnggg! Rrriiinnnggg!

"Mommy, Alex is on top of the refrigerator again," the little girl said, pointing at Alex.

"Let him stay there," Nell grumbled, entering the kitchen. "If he can get his way up there, he can find his way back down." She gave Alex a look that read, *you better not.* Nell recollected the time when Alex saw her approach the refrigerator and used her as a means to soften his landing back down to the floor.

Rrriiinnnggg! Rrriiinnnggg! The phone rang.

Nell lifted the phone's handset from the receiver, positioning it between her shoulder and her ear, "hello?"

"Nell, hi! It's Margo," the voice said.

"Hi!"

"Hi! I wanted to ask a favor. I hope it's okay!"

"It depends; what is it?"

"Okay, it's about the get together next weekend at your place. Paul invited everyone, but he told Cindy that she couldn't come, and that made her very upset."

"Cindy," Nell repeated, her eyes narrowing.

"Yeah, I know it's a big favor to ask, but could she please come? She's been going through a lot lately and we don't want her to feel left out. I know she's Paul's ex, but she's still our friend *and* Paul's. He won't let her come because he doesn't think you would be okay with it. If you could tell him that it's okay with you, then he'll let her come."

What? Uh uh! Nell's eyes became cold and squinted with a curled upper lip. She wanted to slam the phone back down on the receiver. So, Cindy was upset because she couldn't go to *her* house? Why would it be so important for her to be there that day? Was Margo seriously thinking that Nell would casually think it would be okay to invite someone her husband had intimate history with into her home, eating her food, watching their television, and acting like everything was fine? *Unreal!*

"Sorry, I don't think that would be a good idea," Nell said, trying to make her tone not as sharp as it could have been.

"I already told her she could come!"

"What? Why would you do that, after Paul already said no? Why call me after the fact? *That's crazy! She better not come here!"*

"I'm sorry! It's all my fault! Don't be mad at Cindy. Be mad at me."

"I *am* mad at you!"

"Why can't Cindy come? What has she ever done? She's sweet and promised to respect all boundaries. It's no big deal, I promise."

"It's a big deal to *me* and I said no, like Paul did before you ignored what he said too. Why are you still asking?"

There was a long pause at the end of the line. Margo apologized and ended the phone call. Nell wanted to cuss Margo out. Who did she think she was, inviting Cindy over, knowing that neither Paul nor Nell wanted the woman over. That was disrespectful to disregard their wishes to appease someone who didn't live there. Nell wanted to speak to Paul about cancelling the event, but he was looking forward to it and they had already invited their friends. It wouldn't be fair to cancel on everyone else because of his ex and her airheaded advocate.

"You're staying here too?"

"Yeah. I didn't know you were! Aint that something? This is my son, Roscoe. He's five months."

Nell watched as Elsie entered a room two doors away from hers, closing the door behind herself. Nell entered her own room, closing the door. She sat down on the bed. The mattress was hard and firm, but a much better choice than the concrete ground outside. She could hear Roscoe crying from the other room, wondering what was ahead of her when it was her turn to tend to a crying baby. Did Paul receive her letter yet? Was her family in Illinois curious about how she was doing? Did anyone care?

The next day, Nell went to breakfast with the other women and children who were staying at the church. She was grateful to be able to eat a delicious meal prepared by the kind members of the church, reminding her of the family she left behind, resulting in mixed feelings.

"Good morning, Sister Nell," Deacon Seymore greeted her from another table that was filled with some of the church elders.

I guess he's not as uptight as I imagined, Nell thought. I shouldn't be judging people, especially when they were kind enough to take me in. I guess I was just stressed out about being in a new place and being around new people...

"Good morning," Nell replied with a small smile, bringing her fork to her mouth to eat the scrambled eggs that were placed on her plate.

Elsie entered the dining room. She was carrying Roscoe and had dark circles under her eyes. She shifted her son in her arms and carefully grabbed a tray of food.

Frederick entered the facility, making his way straight to Nell's table and sliding into the seat in front of her.

"Mornin', mornin', mornin' to you Sister Nell," he said. "I'm counting on you singing with us today."

Before Nell could object, Elsie approached their table. She put her plate down, shifted Roscoe in her arms, and sat down.

"I'm tired," Elsie complained. "This baby wouldn't stop crying for nothing last night."

"Mornin' Sister Elsie! Hey there, Roscoe, you aint gonna cry around me, huh?" Frederick took the infant into his arms. "Let's let your momma eat in peace. See, babies like me. They always get quiet, like magic."

"How is holding a tired baby magic," Elsie muttered, eating a mouthful of grits. She gawked at Nell. "In a few months, this life will all be yours."

Nell's eyes widened and rolled all the way back to her plate.

"Sister Nell aint much of a talker, is she," Frederick laughed.

Elsie tilted her head to the side and pursed her lips for a second before saying, "she just met everyone yesterday, what could she possibly talk about? What are you up to this time, Brother Frederick?"

"I'm being friendly, is all," Frederick objected. "What's wrong with that?"

"Yeah, I know you're kind of friendly, mmm hmm."

"Don't mmm hmm me. I haven't done anything wrong."

"Mmm hmm."

The pair reminded Nell of her brother and sister. They used to bicker in the same manner and as strange as it was, Nell missed George and Claudine's arguments. Nell pondered if she should give them a call, to see how they were doing. She didn't have to speak to her father and hear another nagging lecture. She wondered if there were any payphones nearby. The call would be long distance and cost a lot of money that she didn't have. How could she contact them, other than writing another letter?

When breakfast had ended, most of the people left to get ready for the upcoming service, leaving Nell alone with a few of the church elders and Deacon Seymore who was preparing to leave himself. He had an office and would be a good person to help her.

Clearing her throat, Nell approached him. For the first time, the deacon welcomed her with a smile.

"Hey, there young lady," he greeted her. "Is there anything I can help you with before service?"

"Sorry to be a bother," Nell said, "but I need to write a letter. Would you happen to have a piece of paper and a pen?"

"Sure, I can spare a few," Deacon Seymore said, leading the way from the dining room. They both walked *to the office area where they entered a room that had a bookshelf, wooden table, executive chair, and religious décor. The deacon opened the desk drawer and handed her two pieces of paper and a blue ink pen to write.*

"Thank you so much," Nell said, her spirit lifted. "This means a lot to me! Thank you! Thank you! Thank you!"

"Anytime, I have more if needed," Deacon Seymore nodded, followed by "yes, lord, mmm hmm."

Nell left the office. She returned to her room to begin writing her letter to her mother and siblings.

Mom, George, and Claudine,

I made it to South Carolina safely. I haven't had the baby yet, but I'm doing fine. I met some interesting people at a local church. They are nosey but seem to be nice and welcoming. I am staying with them for the time being. I am still waiting to hear back from Paul. He's still training, so I'm certain that he will get in touch with me as soon as he can. I'm sorry I had to leave in the way that I did, but I love Paul and want him in my life and the life of our baby. It wouldn't be fair to keep him out of our lives because I know he is a good person capable of loving us with all his heart. I don't care that he is white. Our baby will grow up to love both of us, regardless of who we are. I hope that Dad will understand my decision to leave one day.

Nell

Nell drove Sharon to the Highland Playground, a popular spot where neighborhood children and their families went most weekends. It was popular that day as any other. There were children of all ages laughing and yelping with joy. They were having fun on the wooden see-saws, metal jungle gym, metal merry-go-round, metal slide, metal monkey bars, and much more.

Nell barely opened the door when Sharon took off to join the other children. There were children of different races playing together on the playground, making her recall the time when she was her daughter's age. All her playmates were black, and they rarely interacted with the white children. Everything was segregated with the whites living their lives in their designated part of town and the blacks living in theirs. If either was in the other's space, it meant trouble, *big trouble.*

"Look at me, Mommy," Sharon called out, sitting down on a swing. She began to kick her legs back and forth, making the swing move with the motion.

"I see you, baby," Nell responded, walking closer to stand near the swing set.

"Mommy, mommy, mommy," Sharon sang along, swinging back and forth.

Knock! Knock!
"Come in!"
"Excuse me," Nell said. "It's me again. I finished writing the letter, but I need an envelope and stamp to send it. I would walk to the post office, but it's a long way from the church. Would you happen to have either? I can

give what I can to pay for the items, including the paper. Also, I brought the pen back."

"Don't worry about it," Deacon Seymore spoke, opening the desk drawer to hand Nell an envelope and stamp. "They were sitting there and needed to be used at some point. Yes, lord..."

"Thanks, but I must," Nell said, putting the last of her money on the desk.

"Don't be stubborn, take it all back," Deacon Seymore insisted. "Listen when grown folks tell you something."

"Sorry."

Hesitantly, Nell took back the change, returning it to her purse.

"There's a mail collection box ten blocks away from here," the deacon told her. "I can drop your letter off with the church's. Just leave it on my desk and I'll send it off."

"Really? Thanks!"

Nell wrote her family's address on the envelope and stuffed the letter inside. She licked part of the envelope to seal it and placed the stamp where it needed to be.

"Ten blocks is too far for an expecting mother to walk," the deacon said. "I should know, my wife and I had three young'uns of our own before she passed."

"I'm sorry to hear that. How old are your children?"

"I got three sons. The oldest is twenty-four, the middle one is nineteen, and the youngest is ten. How old are you?"

"Seventeen, but I turn eighteen in a few weeks."

"I remember being seventeen. Yes, lord. I left home to find my own way. I got a job, met my wife, got us a house, and raised our sons. Life was hard, but we made it. Do you have any plans for yourself and your seed?"

"I'm hoping to hear back from my boyfriend," Nell said. "He's on the military base but should be getting out soon. I'm hoping to reunite with him, so we can make plans to raise our baby together. I'm hoping to get on that list for the graduation ceremony!"

"He's the father?"

"Yes, sir."

Deacon Seymore nodded.

"Sounds like a blessing in all aspects: graduation and welcoming a new life into the world. I will be praying for you both and that he does everything that a responsible father should do, which is helping to raise the young'un." The deacon extended his hand and Nell handed him the envelope. He put it in a small pile of outgoing letters.

"Thank you, sir."

"Anytime."

Nell left the office. The church had its front doors open with church members making their way in. Excited, Nell began to picture Paul at the graduation ceremony and how amazing it would be to see him again in uniform. She had never been on a military base before and thought about what it would be like. Her heart fluttered, joyful, like the lively music that was beginning to play. Nell didn't have much on her, but she was happy, happy enough to sing with the choir.

I'm not much of a singer, the young woman thought, but I guess singing a few songs won't be too bad.

Chapter 26

After spending time at the park, Nell and Sharon returned home. Alex was eating from his food bowl.

Sharon made her way to the couch, stretching out to take a nap.

Nell lounged on the loveseat. Thankfully, Paul would return later that day, making Nell feel as if her spirit was glowing. She was glad that she had calmed down a lot since that dumb phone call from Margo. Things had been busy with raising a child and going to school. Yet, Paul had done his best to make sure that the family enjoyed themselves over the weekends, but he was gone for the time being.

Just pretend it's another school day, Nell tried to convince herself, missing her husband.

"Great service, everyone," Frederick told the choir members. "Everyone sang beautifully. Sister Elsie, I don't know what they put in those eggs this morning for breakfast, but the holy ghost certainly went through everyone listening to that solo!"

"Amen, brotha," one of the choir members agreed.

"Ooh wee," Frederick said, his voice energetic. "I'm looking forward to the next service! Everyone stay blessed and be here for the next practice at six Wednesday evening."

Nell had become more excited. Service was entertaining. She enjoyed watching people catch the holy spirit where they would appear to be enraptured, raising their hands, and moving their bodies to the sound of music.

Some moved away from their pews to go up and down the aisles to dance. She had been with the choir and the church for several days. Elsie and Frederick still reminded her of her siblings, but it wasn't as harsh as she had anticipated at first. That was simply their way of being themselves and it didn't bother them a bit.

Nell still had not heard anything from Paul or her family. She wondered if something was going on with the mail services in the area. Maybe if she wrote more letters, they would eventually receive at least one with an encouragement to write back.

"Sister Nell, you got a few minutes to talk," Deacon Seymore asked. "It's important, regarding the letters you've been sending!"

Nell's heart nearly leapt from her chest. Her family or Paul must have written back! It would have been wonderful if she had heard from both! Finally, her efforts would be rewarded! She could hear her family and see Paul! She wished that she had a fancy dress to wear for the ceremony, but all that mattered was the progress!

Nell followed the deacon to his office. She waited eagerly for him to give her the letter or letters! The deacon looked enthusiastic. He sat down to open his desk drawer, removing four letters. He placed them on top of his desk. Thrilled, Nell couldn't help but reach across to grab them, but soon realized that it had been her own letters addressed to her family and Paul, undelivered and unanswered.

What? What is going on, Nell thought, her mind racing, searching for answers.

Deacon Seymore leaning back against the comforts of his executive chair. He stared Nell straight in the face and began to speak.

"Sister Nell," he spoke, "it hasn't been long since you first entered the church and I will have to say, it's been a blessing for everyone here. I've gotten to know you and see that you are a God-fearing young lady who, in a time of temptation, lost her way…You want to beg for your sins to be forgiven, to return home and be with a man who doesn't want to be a father. Has it ever occurred to think that the cycle will repeat itself? I've seen many women in your situation return home, only to be brought back. You are here and should not be fated to return to an unwelcome home or unwanted relationship. I've kept your letters with hopes of offering you a blessing of my own. It is something to seriously consider during these trying times. I can give you a permanent place to stay, at my house. I'll feed and provide for you and your seed, but I want you as my woman. I like that you're young, easy on the eyes, don't talk much, and have a desire to care for others. I need someone who can satisfy my needs, offer companionship, and help around the house. As you know, two of my three sons are fully grown and have moved on with their lives. My youngest isn't that far behind but could use a stepmother who can cook and clean."

Nell froze, her breath also almost being taken away. Regaining her ability to let the man's shocking words sink in, her head drew back quickly. A mixture of fear, disgust, and shock made her heart race. It was unbelievable that the man would act in such a manner, knowing her vulnerability. Eyeing the exit, Nell began to tremble.

"Don't you want to be my wife?" Deacon Seymore asked. "I may be older and not much to look at, but I'm willing to make an honest woman out of you with an opportunity at a decent life. Wouldn't that be better than *being left on the streets? Before telling me no, remember that no young buck is going to want to be with a young woman who has a child that isn't his. You're alone, pitiful, and homeless. Don't be a knucklehead who regrets waiting too long to find a good man because she didn't realize a good one right in front of her face."*

"No," Nell told him, after regaining her composure, "get away from me!"

She rushed out of the office as fast as she could, almost running into Elsie who stepped in the hallway from the women's restroom.

"Sister Nell?" Elsie spoke, watching her almost fly down the hallway.

Nell rushed back to her room, locking the door. She sat on the bed, taking quick shallow breaths. She pushed against the wall, beginning to cry. She wanted to leave the facility, but if she left, where would she go? She had no money and was unable to contact Paul and her family. She was caught between a rock and a hard place.

Chapter 27

"Mommy, I wanna help."

Standing on the tips of her toes, Sharon smiled as she bounced up and down, waiting for permission. They were in the kitchen, preparing dinner for Paul's return.

"Sure, baby," Nell responded. "Let's wash your hands and you can help with the macaroni and cheese. That would help a lot."

Nell helped her daughter up a small stepping stool and helped her wash her hands. She had the little girl join her to add handfuls of shredded cheese to the macaroni. When they finished adding the other ingredients, Nell put on an oven mitt, opened the oven door, and slid the macaroni inside.

"I love macaroni and ch-ch-cheese," Sharon sang. "I love macaroni and ch-ch-cheese. It's really good to e-e-eat. I'd like a whole lot more, p-p-ple-e-e-ease."

Swaying her head from side to side, Sharon waited for the next task, but everything else had been completed. They spent the rest of their time watching television. It wouldn't take long for dinner to finish, so Nell glanced at the clock hanging on the wall to keep track of time.

Knock! Knock!

"Sister Nell?"

Nell stared at the bedroom wall, refusing to respond. She didn't want to talk to anyone. She couldn't believe that at one point she believed she was safe, and that moment, in Deacon Seymore's office, it took every sense of security she had. A lustful man was hungry for her and if he wanted to, he could convince the other members of the church to get rid of her. She was a guest at their facility. Who was she to say something about a man who had been a member far much longer than she?

There were footsteps that became fainter. Nell was hungry, but there was no way on Earth that she wanted to leave the room.

The next day, it was breakfast time. Nell wanted to skip that meal too, but for how long could she go without eating during her third trimester? She was thirsty and her mouth was dry. It had been throughout the night. At least other people would be there, but if one thing was certain, she didn't want to be alone.

Cracking open the door, Nell peered out, seeing two women walking down the hall. Who knew when there would be other people around? As quick as she could, Nell followed them to the dining hall where breakfast was being served.

Unfortunately, Deacon Seymore was there, sitting at a table with other senior members of the church. There was worry on his face, making Nell wonder if he thought that she had already told someone about what he said in the office. He looked at her and began talking to the people at the table.

Nell got in line and received her share of the food. She spotted the table where Elsie and Frederick were, sitting there to join them and the others.

"You okay, Sister Nell?" Elsie asked. "Yesterday, you looked maaaaddd! I knocked on your door to check on you, but you didn't answer. So, I left."

"What?" Frederick gasped. "Sister Nell mad? What did you do, Sister Elsie?"

"Excuse me," Elsie retorted, her head cocked to the side and lips sharp. "I aint did nothin'. It was probably something you did. Anytime there's trouble, your hand's always in it, sir! Uh, huh! Now, the question should be, what did you do this time?"

"Get married already," someone from a neighboring table chimed in.

"It wasn't anybody at the table," Nell said. "I don't want to talk about it…"

"I bet it's that guy you've been waiting to hear from, huh," Elsie puckered her lips." See, men these days aint nothin'. Not a darn one! All the good ones are taken or dead…but guess what, we don't need a man to make us happy. No ma'am! We can do everything ourselves. Why not? We work and take care of the kids anyway."

"Hold on now," Frederick countered. "Why get mad at all guys because of something one guy did? Leave the rest of us out of it! Take some accountability! Nobody forced you to be with the wrong man, my sista."

"Hmm," Elsie rolled her eyes. "Ya'll be nice at first, then change later."

"C'mon, and women don't either?"

"Stop arguing in God's house," someone from a different table told them.

The pair quieted down.

"Good morning, everyone," Deacon Seymore said.

Nell froze. When did he get up and move? Her soul nearly jumped out of her body as the man had the nerve to place his two hands on her shoulders, giving them a firm squeeze. "Sister Nell, good morning…"

Nell lowered her head, struggling not to cry. Deacon Seymore smiled at everyone at the table.

"Remember, Bible study is this Wednesday at 5:30 pm. I look forward to seeing everyone there." He gave Nell's shoulders another squeeze, taking one finger to trail at the lining of her bra. Nell pushed herself away from him, flinching her shoulders. She began to curl her toes.

Elsie squinted her eyes, raising them between Nell and Deacon Seymore who began to walk away as if nothing happened. Sniffling back a sob, Nell left her tray on the table. She went outside to sit in a chair near the entrance. She wanted to ask one of the people in the parking lot if they could offer her a ride to the military base, but remembered that Paul was at a place where she wouldn't be allowed, for the time being. Nell heard that graduation would be in a few days, but since the deacon never sent her letter, chances were that she had no time to get on the list, dampening her spirit. She needed to speak with Paul. She needed his help more than anybody else did. He was smart and always had a plan. With him unaware of the situation, what was Nell to do? She could only imagine how much her father would point out her mistakes, blaming her and Paul at every turn. Where else could she go? She didn't know anybody except the church members and the people at the hotel, but not enough to have anyone offer her room and board for free with a baby on the way.

She shivered, almost tasting vomit in her mouth at the thought of Deacon Seymore touching her again.

"What happened back there?"

Nell turned around to see Elsie standing behind her, her eyebrows drawing together.

"N-nothing," Nell said.

If she were to be thrown into the streets, nobody owed her any favors and if it were her owing them a favor, would it be something distasteful?

"It didn't look like 'nothing'," Elsie said, leaning against a column with her arms folding across her chest. *"Deacon Seymore put his hands on your shoulders, and you looked grossed out...Did he do something?"*

Nell frowned, not saying anything.

"Hmm," Elsie uttered, *"Something aint right, whatever's going on...Keep away from him if he's doing something wrong...You got any other place to stay outside of here?"*

Nell shook her head.

"Maybe you should go back home to your family. Stop waiting for some guy to decide if he wants you back or not. It's not worth it."

"I can't leave without Paul. It's close to his graduation and I can't leave without seeing him. He would be here, if he knew..."

"Paul? That's the whitest name I've ever heard."

"He is..."

"What? Mmm, yep, that white boy's definitely not coming back to be with someone like you... not when he can be with some white girl. You should have known better...And he's the father too? Shoot, he's long gone. Just go back home to your family, raise your baby, and forget about him."

"That's not true and no, I won't! You don't even know him, so who are you to say anything? Where's Roscoe's father? He's black and not here either!"

Elsie put her hands on her hips.

"That's none of your business why Roscoe's dad aint here. What's that got to do with anything? Don't be mad at me when I'm trying to help you out."

The door flew open. Frederick came outside, handing Roscoe back to his mother.

"Hey, you forgot something," he said.

"He's your future son, do your job!"

"Now, I know you lost it! I don't have time for this. I have to go to the college!"

"What ever happened to being good with kids?"

"When I'm not busy, I am!"

"Having three classes aint busy!"

Frederick got into his vehicle, driving away. Elsie giggled.

"It's fun joking around with him. We're at the point where we are doing it for laughs. But back to what we were talking about, go home..."

"I couldn't if I wanted to. I don't have any money. They're in Illinois."

"You could talk to Mrs. Jackson...Maybe she could give you some money to get back home..."

"Maybe," Nell said, squinting. Ugh, why do I suddenly need to go to the bathroom? She rose to her feet, rushing to get to the restroom. Her hips began to ache, forcing her to slow down and crouch towards the floor in the hallway. The pain continued to radiate. "Uugghhh!"

Chapter 28

Nell woke up to the sound of whistling and car keys hitting the kitchen counter.

"Daddy," Sharon's voice was heard.

Nell blinked, rubbing her eyes with her hand. She wondered how long she had been sleeping and if she had done so too long. She jumped to her feet, rushing into the kitchen where Paul stood embracing Sharon. Their eyes met.

"Hey, babe," Paul said extending his arms to kiss his wife. Nell returned the affectionate smooch, her body filling with warmth. "How'd everything go today? Mmm, something sure smells good! Bet I know what it is!"

Oh, no! I forgot about the food! Nell turned off the oven while Paul opened its door to peer inside. The macaroni and cheese was slightly burnt, dampening Nell's spirit a little bit. Paul didn't look too dismayed about it, especially after his stories of eating MRIs in Vietnam.

"Daddy, look at the picture I colored," Sharon spoke, grabbing her father's hand and pulling him towards the refrigerator.

"Oh, wow, look at that," Paul smiled, gazing at his little girl's paper with its colorful scribbles. "I'm so proud! This is, by far, my favorite one yet!"

"I'm gonna make another one," Sharon said, her voice boisterous. She went into the living room to do another.

Paul winked at his wife as he followed their daughter into the other room. He greeted Alex by giving him a quick wink, pointing his index fingers, and giving a playful click of his tongue. The young father strolled deeper into the home, heading to take a shower. Nell wanted to inform Paul about the phone call she received from Margo, but soon decided against it. They both had spoken their peace and that was the end of the story regarding that situation. What really mattered was that Paul was home and everyone was together.

Nell entered the master bedroom to see that the bathroom door was closed with the sound of water running from the shower. She began to hear the muffled sound of her husband humming and singing, bringing a smile upon her face.

Nell burst into tears. She had been admitted to a nearby hospital where she had given birth, naming her daughter Sharon. It had been a few hours since the birth, leaving her exhausted, heartbroken, and confused.

"It would be the best choice," the hospital's social worker told her, "for the baby and yourself. You will have a second chance at a better life to find your own place, get a job, and finish school. Staying at the church isn't a permanent solution. You're still young and can have other children when the time is right. In the meantime, there are plenty of loving couples desperate to offer their love and attention to a little girl who needs a good home. One day, you'll probably meet her again."

But what about Paul and me? What about the love and attention we have to offer our child?

"No," Nell said, "I'm not giving away my baby. I may not have much to offer her now, but I will find a way to make sure that she has everything she needs, even if I have to work day and night."

"Doesn't she deserve to have two loving parents who can properly take care of her?" the social worker asked. "What job do you have where you will be working day and night? Even if you were to get a job, who would watch her? Where would you two live? How can you support a baby when you can't support yourself?"

"Sharon has two loving parents," Nell snapped. "How dare you bring your conniving self into my room talking about taking her away after I almost died giving birth to her! She's hooked up to a machine, barely alive herself! I'm busy worrying about my child! Who asked you to come here to judge me? I've gone through enough! Yes, you're probably just doing your job, but don't you think I've wondered about those questions myself? Those are my problems to solve, not yours or anybody else's! I will find a way for her and me to make it, so don't worry about us! Get out! Sharon's not leaving this hospital except with me, her mother!"

The social worker pinched her lips flat, leaving the hospital room.

Wiping away a tear, Nell sniffled back a sob. she gazed around the room, a sadness dawning upon her. Earlier that day, she had been informed by the doctor that Sharon needed to be placed inside an incubator as a premature baby. Even if Nell was to contact Paul at that time, it was too late to get on the list for his graduation. She would not be able to make it, now that she was stuck in the hospital with a newborn that needed additional medical care. Nell wouldn't be there to reunite with Paul, but she could be there for their daughter.

Sharon's all that I have left, Nell thought. Paul...I tried...I really have...I'm sorry I can't be there for the graduation...I wanted to ...Forgive me...I...I need to be here *for our daughter. People are trying to take her away and I can't allow for her to leave my side…There are perverts out there and she won't be able to defend herself. All she has is me…I will do my best to raise her the best way I can…*

"Hey there," Paul said exiting the restroom. A towel was wrapped around his waist, and he was drying his hair with another towel. "Sorry, but I had to take a quick shower. I didn't want to be all sweaty and ruin dinner."

"It's okay," Nell told him. "I'm just glad everyone is home."

Paul began to dress in his casual clothing.

"Tomorrow will be the last day for this month. Then, during the summer, two weeks for summer camp training. Good thing we have several months until then, huh?"

"Two weeks," Nell repeated, her voice low.

"I'll be back as soon as I can," Paul said. "Then, we can go on a nice family vacation. We'll get a globe, spin it, and go to wherever your finger points to when the globe stops spinning."

"What if it's in the middle of the ocean?"

"We can fish in the middle of the ocean."

"No way!"

"Ok, we'll go to wherever there is land. There! The plan's been modified!"

"Can we afford to do something like that?"

"Sure, I got everything covered. It'll be fun! A family vacation! We'll get cameras and take lots of pictures too."

"I don't think you could spoil Sharon and me anymore than that."

"I want to. It'll be a yearly thing. We could all use a nice trip to create lots of memories. My father used to do the same with my mother, and I plan on doing the same with my foxy wife and my babydoll."

Paul sat down next to Nell who wrapped an arm around him. Paul's plan certainly sounded fun and exciting. Nell and Sharon had never been outside of the country before.

"Paul," Nell said, "I was thinking about the past and it makes me more grateful to be back together. I... I'm sorry I wasn't there for your graduation and sorry for being absent when you got back home from Vietnam. Lots of people were mistreated when they got back..."

"I'm glad to be back too," Paul responded. "I'm not mad at you about not being there. A lot of things happened, and I wish I was there for you as well. My first year in Vietnam was awful. One of our trucks started to have problems on the way back to our camp, so we stayed behind to fix it. Next thing we knew, we were surrounded by the Viet-Cong with their rifles pointing at us. They took us back to a filthy barbwire area in their compound. All we had to eat was one cup of rice and a swig of dirty, brown water each day. It was nasty, but when you're hungry and thirsty enough, you'll eat what is given to you. Most of us got sick from the smell of sweat, vomit, and excrement surrounding us. There were no bathrooms. The ground was as close to one as we could get. I had the handkerchief you had given me. I tried not to get it dirty, but it got filthy because of all the sweat and dirt from my hands and face. It was hard, seeing people get sick and waste away. One guy got so sick, they took him out, and we never saw him again. I had gotten sick myself and was worried about sharing the same fate. One time, I threw up and the guard gave me the same look he had given to the guy who disappeared. He spoke to another guard, and I thought my fate was sealed. I wanted to stay up all night, to remember the good times, wishing I could hold you and be with our baby, but I was so weak, I passed out. When I woke up the next day, the guards were gone. Nobody knows what happened to them, but we were rescued. After I physically recovered, I tried searching for you again in my own way, hitting dead end after dead end. I couldn't take it anymore and started dating again when I never should have. I had gotten short tempered, had nightmares and flashbacks that made me jumpy, violent, and unable to rest. I became the person I never imagined I would be, someone like my Uncle Harry who yelled at and abused his wife. One time, I almost hit a woman I was seeing. I would have done it, if it weren't for her son. The look he gave me when I almost hit his mother, made me realize I was too far gone. I can still see him to this day, the way he stared at me with fear in his eyes. That's when I decided that I couldn't date someone who had kids nor someone who wanted something steady. I guess, I can thank God you weren't around during that time because I wasn't the person from high school nor the person I am now. I was upfront with the women that I wasn't looking for anything serious and they were okay with it. Everyone got what they wanted, until a few wanted more, but I couldn't. I wasn't right for anybody… Things eventually got better… with me slowly regaining control of my life. I'm…better, much better. I'm sorry that I was a monster."

"You're not a monster, Paul," Nell said.

"Shell shock is what they call it," Paul spoke. "I…I'm sorry, Nell. I would have been a horrible husband and father."

"But you aren't," Nell told him. "What matters is the person you are now. The fact that you're remorseful now shows how much you've grown since then. I'm glad you didn't hit the other woman. It…it would have been terrible, as you've said, but I'm sure she forgives you by now. I would like to think so. I'm…I'm glad you're better, Paul. I love you."

"Give me a minute and I'll bring the car around," Frederick told Nell who waited outside.

The doctor released Nell from the hospital, but Sharon had to remain, requiring the use of the incubator. Nell's heart was broken after seeing the newborn inside the machine with all the tubes that showed just how fragile she was. Nell wanted to stay, fearing that her daughter could die or be taken away. She refused to eat and could not sleep. Her body was exhausted, but her thoughts refused to allow her to rest. The doctor had given her pills to help her sleep and they were beginning to kick in when Frederick came to pick her up to drive her back to rest at the church.

My baby will die without me, Nell continued to think, her eyelids slowly starting to get heavier. I can't leave without her. What if I come back and she's gone?

"You look beat," said a young man who looked to be in his late teens. "Are you waiting for someone to pick you up?"

"Yes," Nell yawned, "my ride is on the way."

"I'll stay here until they arrive," the young man said. "What's wrong with this hospital's staff? They shouldn't leave people out by themselves. Anything can happen."

They both waited until Frederick arrived near the hospital's entrance. The young man assisted Frederick in guiding Nell into the car. Nell could barely keep her eyes open.

"Thank you," Nell told the man. "Whatever your name is."

"It's Jack Tillman, ma'am. What's your name?"

"Nell Jefferson."

"Alright, Nell," Frederick said. "We're heading back. Just get some sleep. We'll be back soon to visit Sharon."

"Nell," Jack repeated. "My brother has a buddy who dated a girl with that same name. He said the guy was crazy about her, but I reckon they broke up. She never wrote back to him and didn't show up for visiting day nor the graduation. He was bummed about it."

"Sounds like your buddy needs a new woman," Frederick laughed, restarting the vehicle.

"Tell me about it," Jack chuckled. "Paul deserved better!"

Frederick began to drive away from the hospital.

"Paul," Nell uttered, drowsily.

They stopped at the red traffic light, waiting for it to turn green.

"Paul," Nell spoke again, her eyes dimming.

"Yeah, Paul needs some sense," Frederick agreed.

Nell's body was becoming heavier, especially her eye lids.

Nell struggled to make her eyes open.

Graduation...the base...

"Wait," Nell said, her voice weak. She reached out to Frederick's arm. "Paul...Where's Paul?"

"Huh?"

"W...where's Paul?"

"I dunno. On the base like that guy said."

"Go back!"

"We're heading back to the church. We'll be there soon enough."

"The hospital...I need to find Paul."

"What kind of drugs they got you on?"

"Paul...please...I need Paul...Wait..."

The light turned green.

"Wait," Nell begged, her body weak. "I need Paul..."

The car behind Frederick's blew its horn. Frederick drove ahead but turned the car around. He drove back to the sidewalk near the hospital, observing Jack again who had begun to smoke a cigarette.

"Hey," Frederick called out to him, "I don't know if Sister Nell is hallucinating, but she's been acting strange since you mentioned this Paul character. Now, you said he dated a Nell---wait a minute! Hey, Nell, how do you know, Paul?"

Nell couldn't respond. She fell asleep.

Hours later, Nell awoke to find herself back at the church. She was in her bed in the same outfit she left the hospital in.

Was it a dream, she thought. I dreamt that I ran into a man who said he knew Paul. Was it real or was it the drugs that the doctor gave for me to sleep. I feel so weak...

Nell looked around. She was alone without Sharon, who she soon remembered was still at the hospital. Nell rose from the bed sluggishly. She opened the door to walk down the hallway to the women's restroom. She prayed that Deacon Seymore wasn't near. He would be more than pleased to take advantage of the situation. Nell used the restroom, washed her hands, and headed down the hallway.

"What are you doing out of bed?" Elsie spoke carrying a tray of food in her hands.

"Huh?" Nell asked.

Elsie walked past her, entering Nell's room. She returned to guide Nell back inside.

"I brought the food since Brother Frederick said you were out of it on the way back," Elsie told her. "I've been making sure that nobody disturbed you while you slept. How are you feeling now? You still look tired."

"I need to get back to the hospital," Nell said.

"Why?"

"Sharon...and Paul..."

"That baby ain't goin' nowhere and what of Paul? You still chasing after that white man? Honey, you got more problems than I thought. Eat up! That's why you all messed up now cause you aint got no food in your stomach."

Nell began to nibble at the meal.

"Good, last thing I need to do is spoon feed a grown ass woman," Elsie said. She dug into her pocket and handed Nell a piece of paper. "Brother Frederick said that you were making a fuss back at the hospital and some white man left you his number. What's with you and these white folks?"

Nell looked at the paper that had the name Jack Tillman on it and a phone number. Luckily, the number was local. Slowly, Nell was feeling less tired.

"When is Brother Frederick coming back?" Nell asked.

"There's no telling with him. He comes and goes as he pleases, but he will show up for practice. You need a ride to see your daughter?"

"If he doesn't mind."

"Eh, he'll do it. He likes you. Just don't let Mrs. Jackson see you spending too much time with him. That woman's crazy."

"Why? Isn't she married?"

"That don't mean anything. She can still like someone and not do anything with 'em. Next time when she's around, watch her bugged eyed self whenever Brother Frederick is around."

"But you two hang out all the time."

"I know. That's why she doesn't like me. She thinks I'm interested in him and that we are flirting. That man is like a brother to me and sometimes, to get under Mrs. Jackson's skin, I'll tell Brother Frederick that he's gonna be Roscoe's dad."

Nell smiled, finishing the food from the tray.

"Deacon Seymore hasn't been sneaking around to do anything lately, has he?" Elsie wondered.

"No," Nell said, "I've been in the hospital and haven't seen him in a while. Thank goodness."

"That nasty man is somethin' else. I bet he got worms. Trying to act like he's all religious. Shoot, some people here are as fake as you can get. I'll take the tray back, just this once. Don't expect for this to become a regular thing cause where I'm from, people take care of themselves, and I expect for everyone else to do the same."

"What about Roscoe," Nell countered.

"He's a baby! That don't count, smart aleck."

Elsie exited the room, leaving Nell alone. Fully awake, Nell went to fulfill her duties for the church. She spotted a telephone in the dining room that she had never noticed before. She inquired if anyone would be upset if she were to use the phone to call Jack. She was alone and it was now or never. Nell dialed Jack's number.

"Hello?" the voice answered.

"Hi, is this Jack?" Nell asked.

"Yeah, I was on my way out. Who is this?"

"Nell Jefferson. We met at the hospital. Sorry... I was given some medicine to help me sleep and it kicked in... You know Paul?"

"My brother does. They were friends on the base. So, you're the Nell they were talking about? How come you were at the hospital? Why didn't you respond to any of Paul's letters?"

"I gave birth to our baby not too long ago and just got out. I didn't know about the letters. When did he send them?"

"I have no idea, but I heard he sent a lot out. He even had your name to get on the base for visiting day and graduation, hoping you'd show, but I guess you never got it to know..."

"Do you know if Paul is still on the base? Is there a way I can visit him?"

"No, he's long gone! All the guys are!"

Nell's heart sunk.

"Tell ya what. Paul had a relative that showed up for the ceremony though. He's some big shot in banking. He'd be your best bet."

"Would you know how I could get in contact with this relative?"

"I'll have to ask my dad once he gets home. I can give you a call back. What's this number?"

"I don't know. I'm using the church's phone..."

"Which church is it?"

"Rose Baptist Church on 9th Street."

"I can take a ride up there after work tomorrow."

"Could we meet at the hospital where we met instead?" Nell asked. "A friend will be dropping me off there again tomorrow and I...I need to check on my baby...she's not well and I need to be there for her...Could we, if it's not too much to ask."

"Sure!"

The next day, Frederick took Nell to the hospital to visit Sharon. Later, she met with Jack, who gave her the name of Paul's uncle, Simon Dupont, and an Alabama address and telephone number. Nell attempted to call the number, but all the phone did was ring.

For the next few days, whenever Nell would sneak and attempt to call the number, all it did was ring, frustrating her. All that was left was the address, requiring her to write or make a trip. It would take a long time if Simon chose to respond by mail. A trip to Alabama seemed like her best bet, but it required money, a ride, and the possibility of leaving Sharon, if the doctors felt she needed to stay longer in the hospital.

What if this other relative is like those in Wood Oak, Nell thought. That could put me in a dangerous predicament, and I don't want to put Sharon's life in danger...Going would be risky, especially going alone.

Knock! Knock!

"Come in!"

Nell stepped into the office. Mrs. Jackson was at her desk signing documents. She motioned for Nell to sit down in a chair.

"Yes, what brings you in to see me, Sister Nell?" Mrs. Jackson inquired.

"I need to ask a big favor," Nell said. "As you know, my daughter is in the hospital. I've found a way to get in touch with a relative of my boyfriend, but the number given to me doesn't work...but I have his address. I need to go to Alabama to see him! Is there any way possible that I could get help to go there?"

Mrs. Jackson's eyes narrowed in on her. She took a deep breath, holding it in and gradually releasing it.

"What exactly are you asking," Mrs. Jackson asked, her voice almost raising.

"If I could possibly borrow some money or get someone to take me to Alabama. Once I get back on my feet, I'll pay the money back as soon as I can."

"Alabama," Mrs. Jackson repeated. "How much money do you think this church has? Haven't we done enough? You get free food and a free place to stay. Now, it is anticipated that we will be able to fund free trips so you can be with men while your child is in the hospital?"

"I'm not trying to be a burden. I'm grateful—"

"Close my door on the way out," Mrs. Jackson interrupted, shaking her head and muttering to herself. She resumed completing the work at her desk.

A sob became trapped in Nell's throat.

"I better not have to repeat myself," Mrs. Jackson said, her voice harsh.

Nell wanted to respond, to give the woman a piece of her mind, but she knew she had no option but to leave. She walked away from the woman's office into the hallway. She leaned against the wall. Her eyes began to brim with tears.

"Mmm hmm," Nell overheard Mrs. Jackson speaking over the phone in her office. "That program never should have started cause all we get are these lazy, loose,

and entitled women… Mmm hmm, one just left… Yeah, the one we've been talking about…The baby was just born and already she's trying to make another one. She makes me sick. She thought she would get some church money to fund her sleeping around with some man in Alabama. That was bold asking for money to keep on sinning. I wish I could kick her out… Mmm hmm, right!"

Nell went down the hallway, hearing the music from the room where the choir was practicing. They were singing joyful music, but Nell didn't feel like joining them this time. Obviously, she had overstayed her welcome and had to move. Were there other places for her to go where she would be hired to be able to afford her own place?

"You coming to practice?"

Nell saw Elsie walking her way with Roscoe in her arms. Frowning, Nell shook her head. She couldn't face the woman or anybody else at the moment. Her chest quivering from embarrassment, humiliation, and frustration, Nell hurried back to her room where she burst into tears.

The door slowly opened. Through the blurred vision from her tears, she could make out that Elsie and Roscoe were in her room.

"What's wrong?" Elsie asked. "What happened this time?"

"I'll never see or hear from Paul again," Nell sobbed. "I hope everyone's happy! All I wanted was for my daughter to get to know her father and be with someone who cares about me! Paul wanted me to be there for the graduation, but I couldn't! I'm tired of doing everything I can and having everyone say that I'm not trying hard enough! I fucking am! I'm not lazy, loose, nor entitled, but being with one person makes me that?"

"Wow," Elsie uttered, "you cussing? Someone's mad..."

"Nobody wants me to be happy. I get that! I fucking get it, but why does Sharon have to suffer? Everyone wants to take her away, pointing fingers at me like I'm a terrible mother and some kind of whore!"

"Did that guy from the hospital say that?" Elsie asked.

"No, he helped a lot, but what good is anything if I can't use the information that he gave me? I can't do anything without a stupid ride!"

"Where are you trying to go?"

"To Alabama!"

"Alabama," Elsie exclaimed. "What's over there?"

"Paul's uncle! I need to see him. He's the only link I have."

"How you gonna get to him?"

"I don't know! I guess I'll have to walk there."

"That'll be a long walk. I think you need a better plan."

"So, what! I'll figure out something! Once my daughter gets out the hospital, we're heading that way! In the meantime, I'll see if any nearby businesses need any help with anything for a few dollars. Someone's got to be hiring somewhere."

Elsie sighed deeply. She left the room with Roscoe. Nell exited the room too. She walked outside the building, heading next door to a laundromat. It was a start. There were other buildings in walking distance, and she was determined to find work somewhere. Unfortunately, the laundromat wasn't hiring and neither was the shoe repair business. Nell wished that she had a local newspaper that would tell her specifically who was hiring and also asked *the owners of the businesses if they knew of anyone who was hiring. A local fast food accepted her paper application and said they would contact her in a few days. Nell began to dread the idea of working there, knowing that it would require extensive standing. However, she had a daughter to think about and if they needed her to stand, she would force herself to do so. Nell went to six other businesses before the sun began to set. She returned to the church to finish her usual duties.*

"Sister Nell," Elsie said, reentering the room, "the choir and I are collecting a few dollars to help with that trip to Alabama. If you can wait a few days, we will give you the money collected. Hopefully it'll be enough to get you to where you need to go and back."

"R-really," Nell said, wiping the tears away. "I don't know what to say! Thank you!"

She embraced Elsie.

"Not all of us church folks are bad," Elsie said. "But, let's just say, some of us can understand."

For the next few days, Nell visited her daughter in the hospital, and took odd jobs around the area and from a handful of church members such as babysitting, cleaning, and helping the elderly. Nell wasn't sure how much money the choir had collected, but she was grateful. It brought her steps closer to her goal.

Tired, Nell finished her duties at the church, collapsing down on the bed. Everything was getting busier, but she didn't care. Also, the doctors said that, soon, Sharon would be well enough to leave the hospital. Making things more fruitful that progress was finally being made. Nell stretched in the bed. Her gown was slightly damp, but she was so tired she didn't care. She rolled to her side, dozing off.

Then, the door creaked open and closed.

Nell rolled to her other side, making out a shadowy figure near the door of the room. Her heart racing, Nell flicked on the lamp's light, nearly screaming at the sight of Deacon Seymore standing in her room.

"Shh," Deacon Seymore spoke.

"What are you doing here?" Nell demanded, pushing herself upright against the head of the bed. "Get out of here!"

"Stop making all that racket," Deacon Seymore spoke in a stern audible whisper. His face was pinched before speaking further. "Let's make a deal. I heard that you're in need of money. I have plenty and then some! I'll pay whatever the price, but I want something in return. Your baby is still in the hospital and your breasts are full and leaking. If you give me a drink, it's easy money and wouldn't be any different than feeding your child, only it'll be me."

Nell's top lip curled in revulsion. Deacon Seymore's words made her feel unclean with the strongest urge to vomit. Acid almost to her throat, Nell nearly gagged before shouting, "No! Get away from me! Get out of this ro—!"

The deacon rushed forward covering Nell's face with his large hand, pinning her against the head of the bed. Nell's screams were muffled by the deacon's hand. Nell grabbed at the deacon's hand to remove it. Her nails dug into his skin. Deacon Seymore let out a shriek before grabbing Nell's neck and forcing her down between the edge of the bed and the wall. He struck her with his fist twice, pinned her down with an arm, and yanked Nell's blouse upwards, exposing her bra. Quickly, the deacon pulled the bra down, cupping one of Nell's breasts in his hand. He squeezed it before leaning forward with his mouth open.

"Help," Nell screamed, kicking, and hitting the deacon. "Somebody help!" She grabbed onto the deacon's ears, pulling his face away from her.

"Shut up," the deacon ordered her, lifting his hand to strike once more. Nell kicked him between his legs, causing the man to release a cry of agony. He reached down to cover his groin. With the man reeling in discomfort, Nell attempted to escape, but the deacon's heavy body was still partially on top of her. Accidentally, Nell kicked the nearby nightstand, causing the lamp to move. Intentionally this time, she did it once more, causing the glass lamp to shatter on the floor.

"What's that noise?" a faint voice outside the room asked. "Did something break?"

"Sounds like it came from one of the bedrooms," a distant voice responded.

"I'm so tired. I've been cleaning all evening..."

"Help," Nell gasped.

The deacon recovered enough to begin covering Nell's mouth with his hand, waiting for the other women to pass.

"Has anyone seen Nell?" Elsie's distant voice was heard.

"You're gonna pay for that," Deacon Seymore told Nell. "All this trouble, I might as well go all the way." His hand pressed harder against Nell's face. Tears began to fall heavily from Nell's eyes, hearing the sound of the deacon unzipping his pants with his other hand.

There was silence, then the sound of footsteps getting closer to the door. Nell attempted to scream, but all that came out was a low muffled sound.

"Sister Nell?" Elsie's voice called out from the other side. "Are you in there? Hey, her door is locked! Sister Nell! We heard a crash. Are you okay? Someone get the key!"

The deacon began to cuss. He faced Nell, giving her a serious look.

"You say anything, and you're finished, you and that damn baby, you hear," he warned Nell. He crept to the wall near the door's entrance, pressing his back against the wall.

The door opened. Elsie and another woman stepped inside.

"Sister Nell," Elsie said, "are you okay? There was a crash and we wanted to check on you."

"Deacon, what are you doing here?" the other woman exclaimed, spotting him with his back against the wall at the entrance.

The other women began to gasp, pointing.

"He attacked me," Nell told the women. "He's tried to force himself on me!"

"That's not true," Deacon Seymore countered. "I was here to give Sister Nell money like everyone else, but she wanted more and offered herself. When I said no, she vowed revenge, threw the lamp on the floor, and screamed."

"That's a lie if I ever heard one," Elsie said, putting a hand on her hip and pointing a finger at the man. "Why was the door locked? Why would you give her money at this hour all by yourself? Why is the zipper on your pants unzipped? You a dirty ass n*****!"

"Someone call the police!"

"Nell, are you okay?"

"The deacon's a pervert!"

"Babe?"

"Huh?"

"Is everything alright?"

"Sorry, I zoned out. Um, I talked to Margo earlier today. She wanted Cindy to come over. Is it okay that I said no?"

"Sure! They'll eventually get over it."

"It's just…She's your ex and…will this make things awkward with your other friends?"

"Nope. Boundaries are boundaries. Cindy's asked me to not come over when she started dating a guy or two."

"Really?"

"Yeah, and we usually ended up back in that on again, off again pattern. But this time, it's staying off for good."

"Aren't we on and off too?" Nell scoffed.

"Well, not to that extent and it was different circumstances."

"Remember when we had a talk about having a second baby?"

"Yeah?"

"I'm scared of relying on others and being vulnerable again. Sometimes when people see that you have nothing, some try to take advantage."

"If anything happens to me, you and Sharon will be very well taken care of. I made sure of that."

"Yeah, but I don't want anything to happen to you…I just want everyone to be safe and secure."

"We are. I'm trying the best I can."

Nell sighed, frowning.

"Nell, I don't know what more I can do," Paul sighed.

Chapter 29

Finally, the weekend came when the Boudreauxs were to have the gathering at their home. The neighbors, including the Reeves, attended. Nell's study group came, as well as Paul's friends. Awkwardly, Cindy arrived, uninvited, with her son, Jacob.

What is she doing here, Nell thought, almost balling her hands into a fist and wanting to smack the woman across the face.

Cindy was talking to another guest on the front porch. Both were laughing and talking. In Cindy's hands was a covered blue bowl.

"Nell, hi," Cindy spoke, giving Nell a smile that couldn't have been more fake.

"Hi," Nell said, through her slightly grinding teeth. "I thought that Margo was supposed to talk to you."

"She did, but I think we can work things out," Cindy said. "I would like for us to be friends. Paul and I still are, so we can be too."

Nell gave the woman a flat look, crossing her arms over her chest.

"Is Paul friends with any of your exes?" Nell asked Cindy, her voice taking a tart tone.

"No, but—"

"Why are you here?"

"Cindy," Margo exclaimed coming from the inside of the home and embracing Cindy, "you made it!"

Nell cocked her head to the side.

"Excuse me," Nell interrupted. "Why is everyone acting like I'm not here? Uh uh!" She shook her head, at her wits end. She marched into the home searching for Paul. Not only did Cindy have to go, but Margo too! Who did those women think they were? Whose house did they think they were in? This was Nell's home, not Cindy's! She scanned the home, not seeing her husband within the crowd inside. Nell marched outside, spotting Paul who was joking around and manning the outdoor grill. Greyson stood nearby drinking a glass of lemonade. The outdoor guests were relaxing on the outdoor furniture, eating, talking, or watching the football game on the portable television set.

"Paul, we need to talk," Nell told her husband.

"Sure," Paul replied. "What about?"

"Cindy's here," Nell whispered, her tone harsh.

"What?" Paul responded, his voice disbelieving. "Where is she?"

Nell led her husband back to the front entrance, but Cindy and Margo weren't there. Nell heard laughter coming from the dining room. She stomped there, spotting Cindy and her stooge of a friend, Margo, at her side sampling what seemed to be a homemade cheeseball from Cindy's blue bowl with potato chips that Nell had purchased!

"Paul, hey," Cindy smiled upon seeing them.

"Cindy, you need to leave," Paul told her.

"And you too," Nell told Margo.

"I thought we were friends, Paul," Cindy reminded Paul. "I don't see what the big deal is. I brought the cheeseball you like."

"It's about respecting our wishes," Paul countered. "You could have joined everyone next week at Tom's."

"Why not *this* week," Margo chimed in. "Everyone's together *today*! Cindy's been with the group much longer and shouldn't be ostracized because Nell's insecure. How would being at Tom's place be any different from today? Shouldn't everyone get along?"

"This is my house, not hers," Nell reminded her adversary.

"Actually, it's *Paul's* house too," Cindy argued. "Doesn't he have a say?"

"He just said to leave!"

"Only because *you* did. What about what he really wants?"

"What do you mean by what he really wants?"
Paul groaned briefly.

"Listen," he said firmly, his eyes more stern than usual, "Cindy, this home belongs to Nell and me. If you are asked to leave, it shouldn't be that hard to do! Instead, you chose to come here uninvited. What did you expect was going to happen other than an argument?"

"So, would it be okay if you and Nell couldn't come to our homes either?" Margo stated.

"Sure! We could always stay here or go to someone else's place to watch the game. It'll be fun regardless for us. In fact, I'm looking forward to it!"

"But, Paul--," Cindy whined, her voice cracking. The woman burst into tears. She quickly left the room, got her son, and made her way out the front door. Margo took off after her friend.

Nell made her way to the master bedroom. She wanted to tell everyone to leave and never leave the room again. Paul followed her, closing the door behind them and locking it.

"I'm sick and tired of Cindy," Nell told her husband. "She has a lot of nerve coming here after we both told her not to come!"

"Calm down...She's gone."

"You sure can pick 'em, Paul! How many more messed up women from your past are gonna keep coming back? Is there a reason why Cindy was here today that I don't know about? Did you invite her over?"

"No! I knew something like this would happen. That's why I told her not to come."

"What about the time after the art show? Are you still sleeping with her?"

"What? I wouldn't do that!"

"Yes, you would! While I was alone and struggling with our daughter, you were busy running around town sleeping with every woman in sight! No wonder you caught something!"

Their eyes met with Nell seeing resentment and hurt in her husband's eyes. Paul left the room, leaving her alone. Nell wasn't sure how to feel. She hated viewing a reminder that Paul had been with someone else. Was he keeping Cindy around, in case they broke up? Did he leave to chase Cindy down and have sex with her as a form of revenge? Margo certainly would have approved of that notion. Did anyone care about Nell's happiness? Maybe Paul did love Nell but wanted someone else too. It wasn't fair. Nell didn't want to share her husband with anybody else. She had heard about swingers, but there was no way she wanted to be a part of that lifestyle, but, maybe Paul did.

Laying down and hugging a pillow, Nell curled into a fetal position. She began to sob, wondering how much of a string her marriage was being held by.

The deacon was taken away by the police. Nell had already given her statement. After hearing what had happened, Frederick volunteered to take Nell down to Alabama to see Simon Dupont. Sharon remained in the hospital. Most of the drive was quiet, but seeing the trees, lakes, and other greenery cheered her up some. The drive was lengthy, but finally, they arrived at what seemed to be a winding road in a heavily wooded area, ending the drive at a brilliant metallic gate that was guarded.

"May I help you?" the security guard asked.

"Yes, is Paul Boudreaux or Mr. Simon Dupont here?" Nell asked from the passenger side of the vehicle.

"What is your name? Mr. Dupont isn't expecting any visitors today."

"I'm Nell Jefferson. I'm Paul's girlfriend. I need to see him or speak with his uncle."

"Mr. Boudreaux is not here, and you say that you're his girlfriend? I will call the main house to see about your visit," the guard said.

Nell and Frederick waited, only for the guard to return to the vehicle with a shake to his head.

"I'm sorry, but Mr. Dupont will not see you."

"What about Paul?" Nell asked. "When will he be back? Do you know when we can come back to speak with him?"

"Ma'am, you must leave the grounds right now. Mr. Dupont has ordered for me to call for your arrest, if you and your friend stay any longer."

"But, I need to speak to Paul or find a way to get in touch with him! Please!"

"We're leaving," Frederick said, turning the car around and driving away.

Nell began to sob heavily.

"This has got to stop," Frederick told Nell. "Stop being so stubborn for once in your life! Them white folks don't want anything to do with you or your baby! Call and go home to your kinfolks. They will take you in."

Nell remained silent until they came across a phone booth. Frederick parked his vehicle, handing her some change from his front pocket.

"Call your folks, right now," he spoke.

Reluctantly, Nell went inside the booth. She looked into the sky, remembering the fight she and Mr. Jefferson had.

"He got his diploma," Nell recollected her father yelling. "What do you have? Nothing except his baby that he will probably abandon too once another cute little thing comes his way. You want to be on welfare like all the other girls who have nothing because they were too stupid to not keep their legs closed? It's either him or us! You better choose wisely because once you leave, don't think of ever coming back!"

I can't, Nell thought. It'll only make things worse. I…I want to just die, but I can't leave Sharon alone…What if they take her away or some pervert tries to abuse her, like they've done to me or worse? What can I do?

Then, Nell remembered Holiday's Garage, a place where Paul had worked previously. Maybe they would know something. She dialed 0, spoke to the phone operator, and placed the coins into the coin slot. The operator soon connected her to Paul's former place of employment.

"Holiday's Garage," a voice spoke.

"Hi," Nell said, "I'm trying to get in touch with someone who used to work there. His name is Paul Boudreaux."

"Paul left months ago! He's a cool and hardworking guy that Mr. Holiday wanted to keep around!"

"I know... Does he ever call there or has any plans to visit?"

"Hmm, well, every once in a blue moon, Paul will call. He called a few days ago to check on everyone and told us about how he graduated from some military base in South Carolina, but he didn't leave an address or number. There's no telling when he'll contact us again, but if he's heading to Vietnam, it'll be a long while."

"Please, I'm begging. I need to reach him and there is no other way but here. May I write to him with your address and have the letters forwarded to him? It's very important..."

"Sure, but may I ask who you are?"

"I, uh..."

"This has got to stop," Nell remembered Frederick saying to her. *"Stop being so stubborn for once in your life! Them white folks don't want anything to do with you or your baby!"*

"I...I'm just a friend," Nell said, choking back a sob. She jotted down the address to Holiday's Garage and walked back to Frederick's vehicle. *A friend...I guess that's what I am, if that...I wanted to be more, but how can a relationship be called that if there's only one person? Paul...I love you. How long must I wait? Is there anything worth waiting for? I need to stay strong and at least fix my own life for the better. I have to, for Sharon. She's here and needs me to be strong. I must think of her future as well. I'll find a way to finish school where I'll never have to rely on anybody else ever again, including you.*

The door to the bedroom reopened. Paul slipped inside, closing it behind himself. He slid into the bed, spooning his wife with his arms wrapped around her.

"I told everyone you weren't feeling well," Paul said, "so Greyson's manning the grill and Joel's keeping things in line inside. I wanted to be here with you."

"Why," Nell sniffled. "Cindy didn't want you this time?"

"No, I wanted to be with my wife because I love her. Nell, when I say that I love you, I mean it. I only say those words to people I genuinely care about. You and Sharon hear it all the time because I mean every word."

"It meant nothing when you were with those other women."

"I'm sorry. I will always be sorry, but in all fairness, I haven't been with anybody else since we got back together. I mean, why would I when I have my dream girl right here?"

"I'm not your dream girl," Nell grumbled.

"Yes, you are!"

"Well, I don't hear anything about you being with any other black women."

"What makes you think that?"

"You did?"

"Yeah, but like the white women, they weren't you. Does it really matter?"

"No, I guess not. I'm sorry, if I got you and your friends in a rough spot."

"Nah, some need to understand boundaries. They'll be mad for a bit, and we'll all go back to the way things were before, only there's a new sheriff in town."

"Me?"

"Yep," Paul chuckled, kissing her shoulder. "Speaking of keeping things in line. I gotta apologize to someone for what happened in the parking lot, since he was innocent and all."

"You're gonna apologize to Martin, someone you disliked since high school?"

"It wasn't him. It was his old lady. He still didn't have to blab about my medical history, but he didn't key Wilma so, I'll apologize for at least that part."

"That's strange coming from you."

"I know, but at least I'll give it a go."

They continued to snuggle until Nell felt better enough for them to rejoin the gathering.

Chapter 30

Rrriiinnnggg! Rrriiinnnggg!

"I'll get it," Nell told Paul. She wiped her damp hands against her apron.

The gathering at the Boudreaux home had been successful with most of the attendees getting along, minus the incident that occurred earlier that day. Surprisingly, there wasn't much to clean with most guests taking care to clean behind themselves. Paul had taken out the trash bags and began to clean the outdoor grill. Nell cleaned the dishes that would need to be returned to their owners. When it came to Cindy's blue dish, Nell was tempted to hurl the darn thing into the trash.

"Hello," Nell answered, pressing the phone's handset between her shoulder and ear.

"Nell, it's Cindy," the voice said.

Cindy! Uh! I'm so sick of that woman!

"I'm sorry about showing up uninvited," Cindy said. "But it hurt my feelings that I wasn't invited and everyone else was. What did I do to be singled out?"

"I don't want my husband's ex coming over," Nell stated.

"But why is it okay that I invited you both to the art show and you both attended, but when it comes to the football game, I can't attend? How would this be any different than going to anybody else's house?"

"I didn't want to go. I only went because Paul wanted to support you and have me be there. I didn't want you here today because I don't trust you with him. What you and Margo did today confirmed that neither of you respect me enough to care about boundaries when it comes to my marriage to Paul. So, how am I to trust either of you after that?"

"Paul is my friend."

"Yeah, and he is my husband. I have no problems with him having friends, but let's be clear on a few issues. He is married and the position of being his wife is filled, with no upcoming vacancies. As his friend, yes, you are entitled to your feelings. However, as his wife, I am entitled to mine too and mine are to be respected by him and people who call themselves his friends because if you are truly his friend, you'd care about him and the family he cares about."

"Okay..."

Nell waited to see if Cindy had more to say, but the phone call ended.

Chapter 31
Paul

The following day, Paul waited in the clinic's parking lot. There, he saw them, Martin and his girlfriend, Dr. Washington, walking from the clinic's back doors. They looked happy, but the tone quickly shifted when Paul exited his own vehicle, making the pair stop in their tracks.

Dr. Washington turned to Martin, grabbing his arm, and attempting to pull him back towards the building.

"I'm here to talk," Paul called out, keeping his distance.

"With your fists again, huh?" Martin responded, keeping a close eye on his enemy. "Mabel, go back inside and get security."

"I'd like to talk with her too," Paul said.

"Your business is with me, not my woman," Martin told Paul. They both waited until Dr. Washington was back inside the building.

"There was a misunderstanding," Paul told Martin. "My friends and I thought you were the person who keyed my car, but it turns out, it was your old lady…"

"What of it? You want to beat her up? Not on my watch!"

"Listen, I'm not here to beat her up, okay! I'm here to apologize for the fight in the parking lot that day…and for all that went on in high school…I shouldn't have done the things I did back then either…I know an apology can't change things, but I'm sorry for the person I was in high school and the person I was that day in the parking lot…"

The back door to the clinic reopened with a security guard stepping out alongside Dr. Washington.

"Sir, you need to leave the premises," the guard told Paul.

"Hold on, Troy," Martin told the guard. "Give us another minute or two."

Paul turned to Dr. Washington.

"Even though you ruined my car and blabbed about personal matters... thanks for curing me of my ailments. I wouldn't have wanted to pass it on to another innocent person, especially my wife...I...I'm trying to be a better person."

Paul cleared his throat. He reentered his vehicle and drove away from the clinic. He wondered if Martin would forgive him, and deep down, if he would forgive himself. The young man drove to the nearby lake and parked his car.

"Hello, old friend," Paul said, his voice barely audible. "Good to see you again."

Many times, Paul thought about doing more, driving further into the lake until Wilma and he were no more, but he was glad that he waited. His prayers had been answered, to have Nell and his daughter back, and another chance to change his life for the better. It was still a work in progress, but he was closer than he had been previously. He had stepped back so many times but could now say that he had taken a few steps forward.

Reaching down to the front passenger seat, Paul grabbed the package that had arrived the day before. It had been sent to him from Stephen Barnes, his friend from Wood Oak, Louisiana. The package contained two yearbooks and a letter.

Paul,

I hope you are well. I was finally able to get the original yearbook back from Nancy. Actually, I got Doris to get it back when she and a few other people went to Nancy's place for a bachelorette's party. It's in rough shape, but it has the signatures of a few classmates who are no longer here, including two classmates who passed away. I'm sure you'd appreciate them. I got the second book from our old librarian. She gave me the last copy she had because the original had been stolen by your ex. I tried to get as many signatures as I could. I'll keep in touch! Take care, buddy!

Stephen Barnes

Paul looked at the first yearbook. The front and back cover were gone. The first few pages had been ripped out. The pages that did remain were torn but contained many signatures and messages. Unfortunately, they had been scratched and scribbled over by a black pen or marker. Paul was barely able to read through most of the scribbles. Squinting his eyes, he was able to make out a few messages.

Paul,
You are a great friend, and I will always cherish our friendship. You are one of the liveliest people I've ever known! Keep that winning smile and friendly personality for that's what makes you the popular person you are! I'll never forget you! May God bless you in everything you do!

Love ya!
Gloria Dearman

Paul,

Remember Mr. Hall in the 10th grade? We had a really good time in that class! It's been a very interesting past four years! Best of luck in everything you strive for!

Jane Walters

His eyes brimming with tears, a smile took over Paul's face. His chest had an expanding feeling.

Paul,

In any situation, you're a swell guy! I'm certain you'll make it fine after leaving here because you're a wonderful person!
Daniel Harris

Paul,

Always stay as fun to be around as you are now, ya hear! I enjoyed going to school with you for the past four years! I'll always remember the sock hops, the games, and the laughs! I don't think I could have a better friend anywhere if I tried. We'll always keep in touch!
Stephen Barnes

If you're ever in New Orleans, come see us! We enjoyed knowing you at Wood Oak High School!
Travis and Thomas Nicholson

Dearest Paul,

**I hate to see the fun and laughter come to an end!
You're so amazing and I'll never forget you!**
Ellen Parnell

Thanks guys, I appreciate reading this more than you can possibly imagine, Paul thought, flipping through the yearbook to see what other messages and pictures he could make out. There were more torn and scribbled over messages throughout the book. Eventually, Paul came across the senior pictures of the class of 1970. The page that would have contained his picture had been ripped out. He turned to the page that would have contained his wife's picture, but her entire image had been erased clean, including the section where her name would have been printed. Unfortunately, there was something handwritten in Nancy's handwriting written above the erasure of what would have been Nell's image. It said one word, n*****. Martin's name and image shared the same fate, leaving a bitter taste in Paul's mouth.

The young man reached over into the glove compartment, pulling out a black ink pen. He scratched out the vulgar words, writing both Nell and Martin's names down into the area where the names had been erased and what was left of the boxes containing the erased images.

Paul began to browse through the second yearbook. It contained many heartfelt signatures and messages. The young man was happy to see himself in a good number of pictures, flooding his mind with many memories.

Martin was in a few pictures himself, most being in the science class. That brought a chuckle to Paul's heart and mind, knowing the secrets that occurred in the classroom before and after school between his wife and himself. Those were the most interesting times that never made the yearbook! Paul searched the book for more images of his wife, but other than her senior photo, there was only one: her sitting alone at a table in the cafeteria.

"I'm sorry, babe," Paul whispered, closing his eyes with a heavy sigh. He reopened his eyes, touching the image of his wife. With his pen, Paul drew a figure sitting next to her, writing his own name next to the figure. He flipped the pages back to the senior photos, ending it where his wife's photo was. At the end of the name, Nell Jefferson, Paul wrote, "—Boudreaux," along with a message.

My darling wife, because of you I've grown to become a better and stronger person in more ways than I could possibly imagine. I love you and always will, with my entire being.

Paul

Epilogue

Paul returned home to find his wife in the backyard with Sharon and Alex. He told her about the second yearbook. He said that they would share it, and that she had a message inside next to her senior picture. After reading it, Nell smiled at her husband, giving him a quick smooch. She went inside the home with the book and returned outside minutes later. She handed Paul the yearbook, opening to the page that contained his senior photo. Next to his picture was a handwritten note that read:

**Paul, my husband, my bad boy, my lover,
It's been a long, bumpy journey, but if I had to do it with anyone, I'm glad it's with you. I love you too, always and forever.**

Nell

Love Fumbles 4

Coming Soon

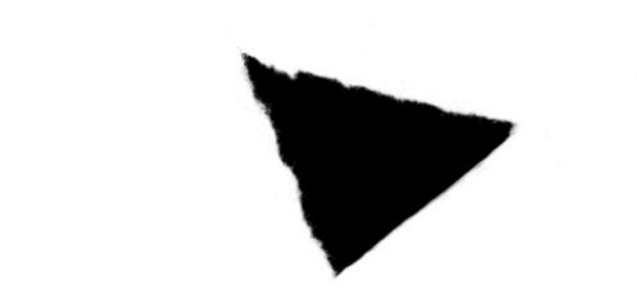

9 7 9 8 9 8 5 4 6 4 8 4 9